SUPERHERO ABC

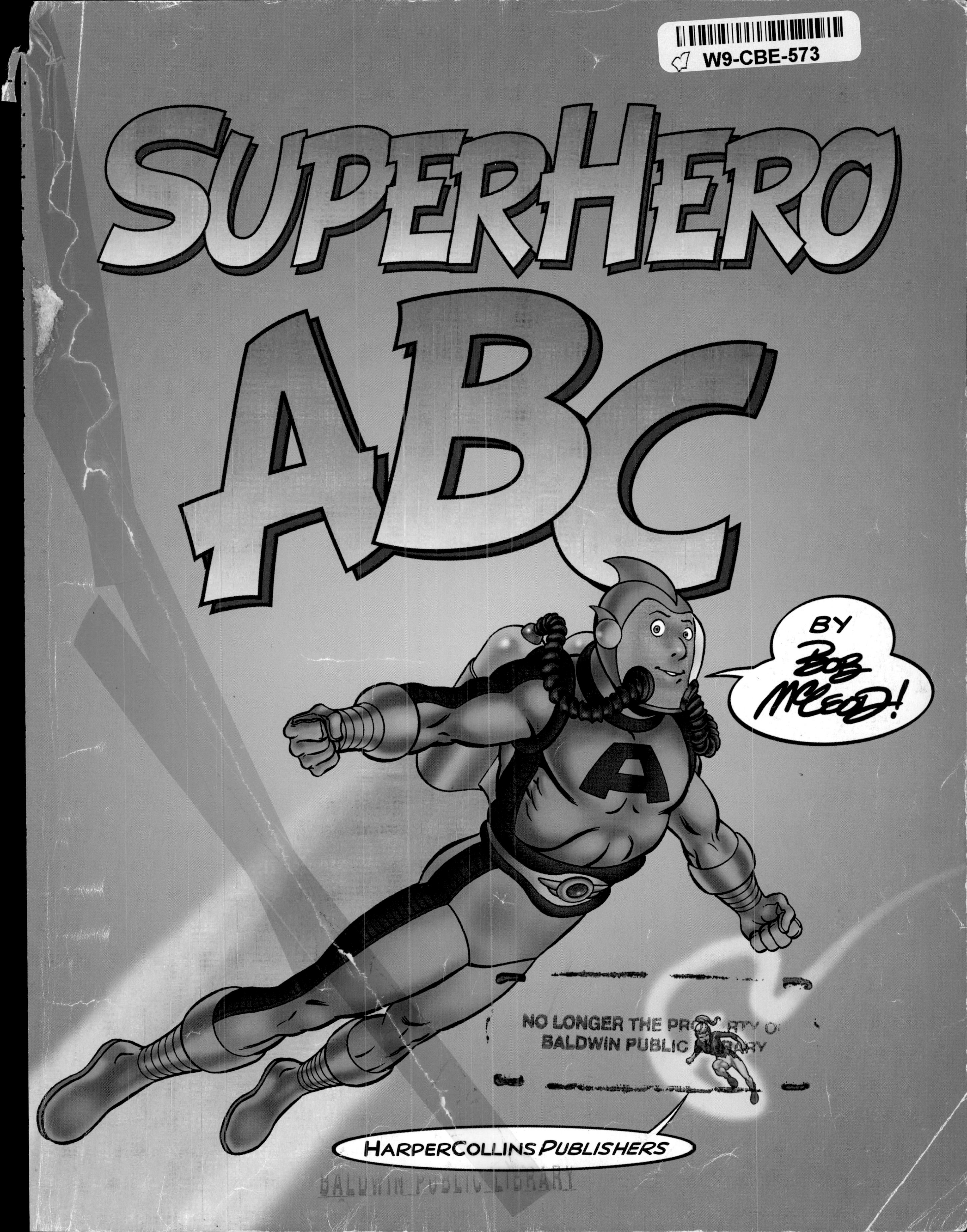
BY BOB McLEOD!

HARPERCOLLINS PUBLISHERS

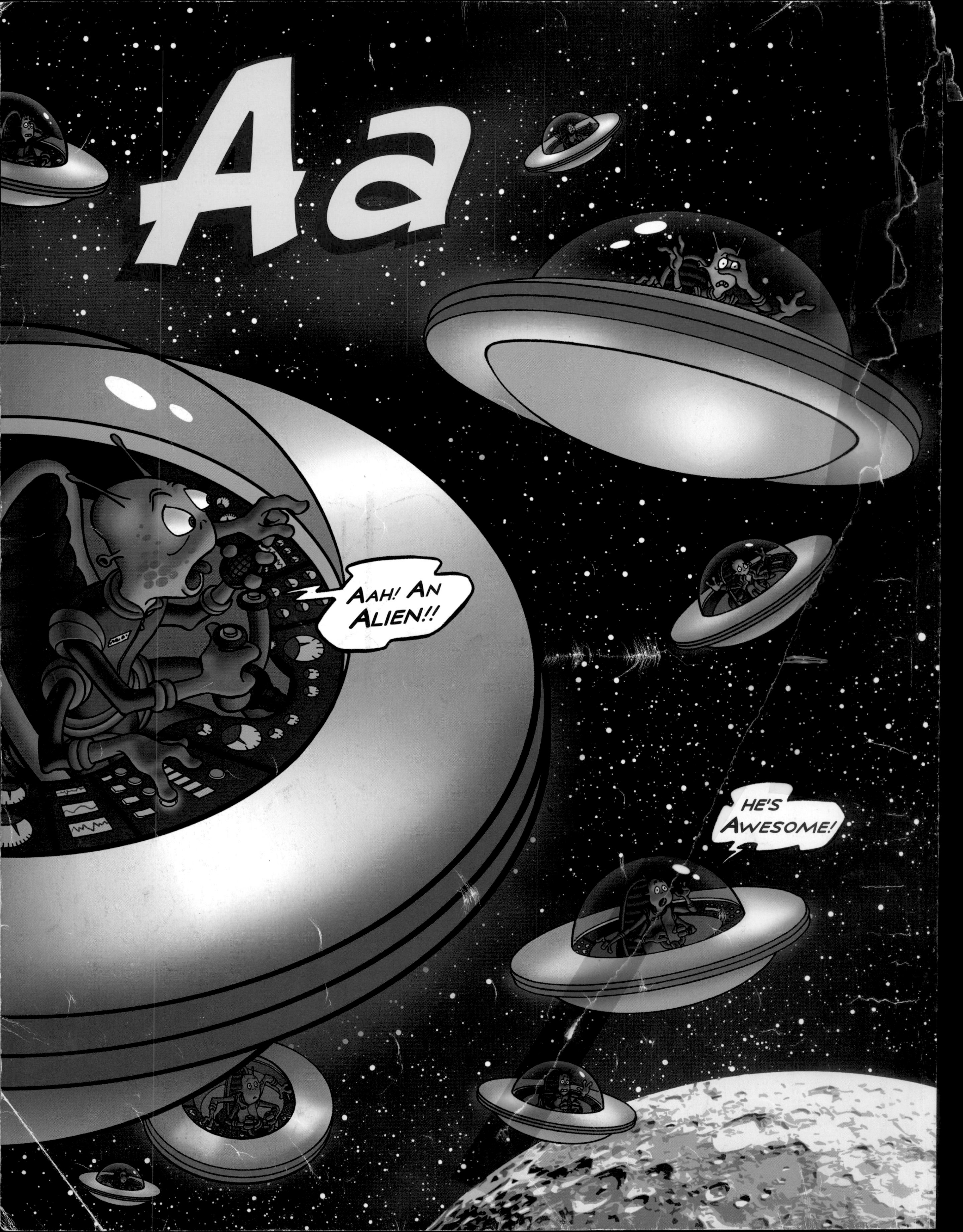
Aa
AAH! AN ALIEN!!
HE'S AWESOME!

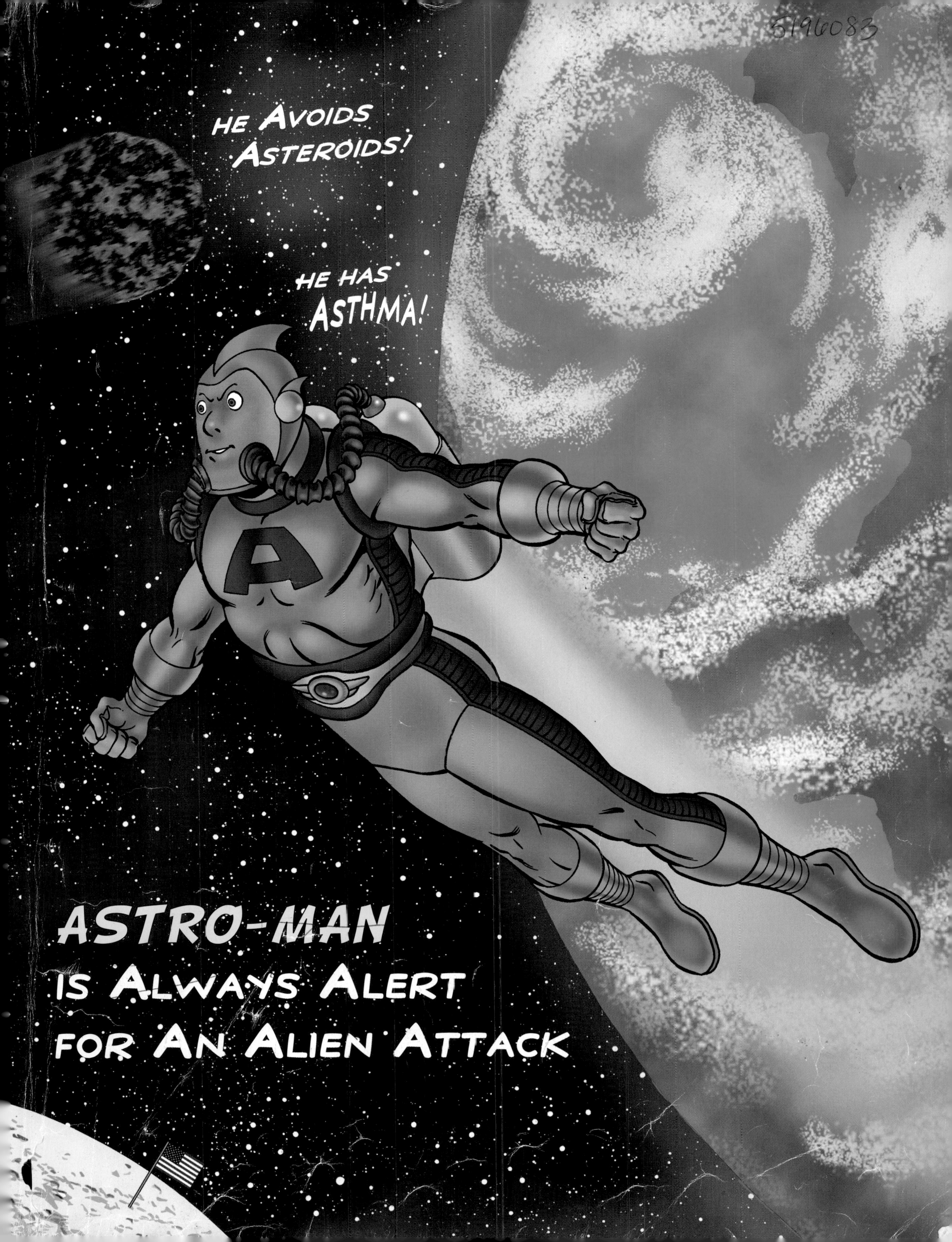

HE AVOIDS ASTEROIDS!
HE HAS ASTHMA!
ASTRO-MAN
IS ALWAYS ALERT FOR AN ALIEN ATTACK

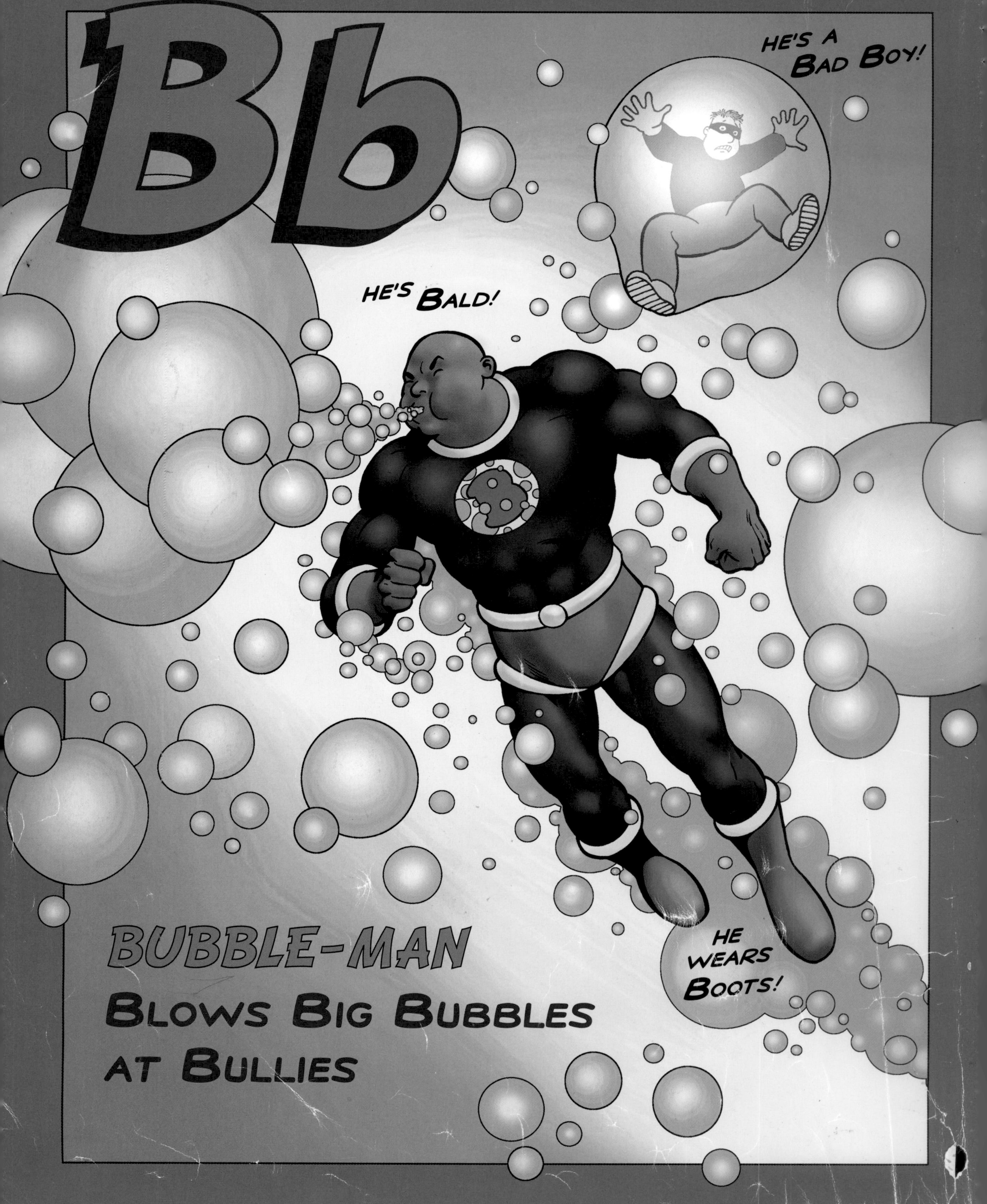
Bb
HE'S A BAD BOY!
HE'S BALD!
HE WEARS BOOTS!
BUBBLE-MAN
BLOWS BIG BUBBLES AT BULLIES

Cc

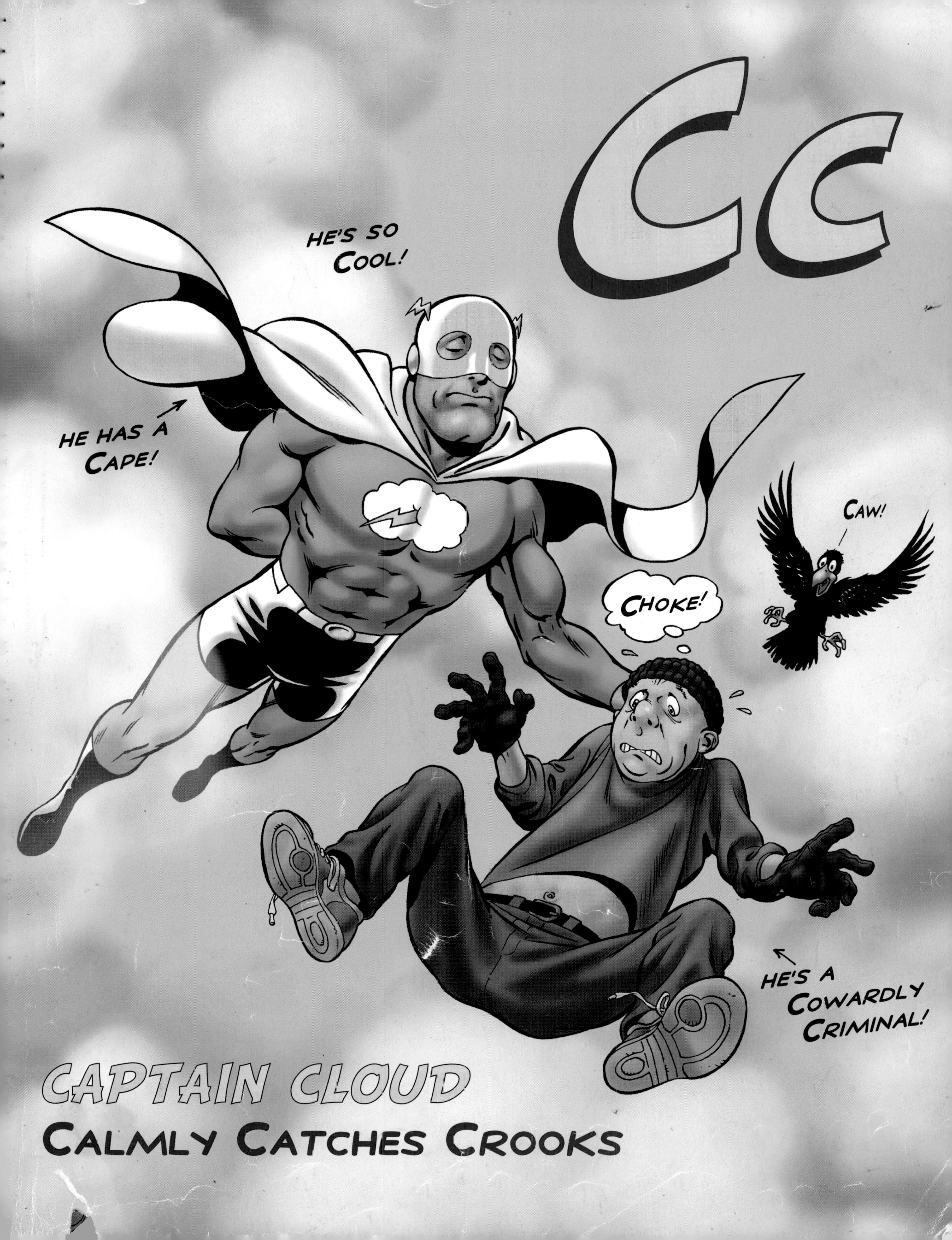

HE'S SO COOL!
HE HAS A CAPE!
CAW!
CHOKE!
HE'S A COWARDLY CRIMINAL!

CAPTAIN CLOUD
CALMLY CATCHES CROOKS

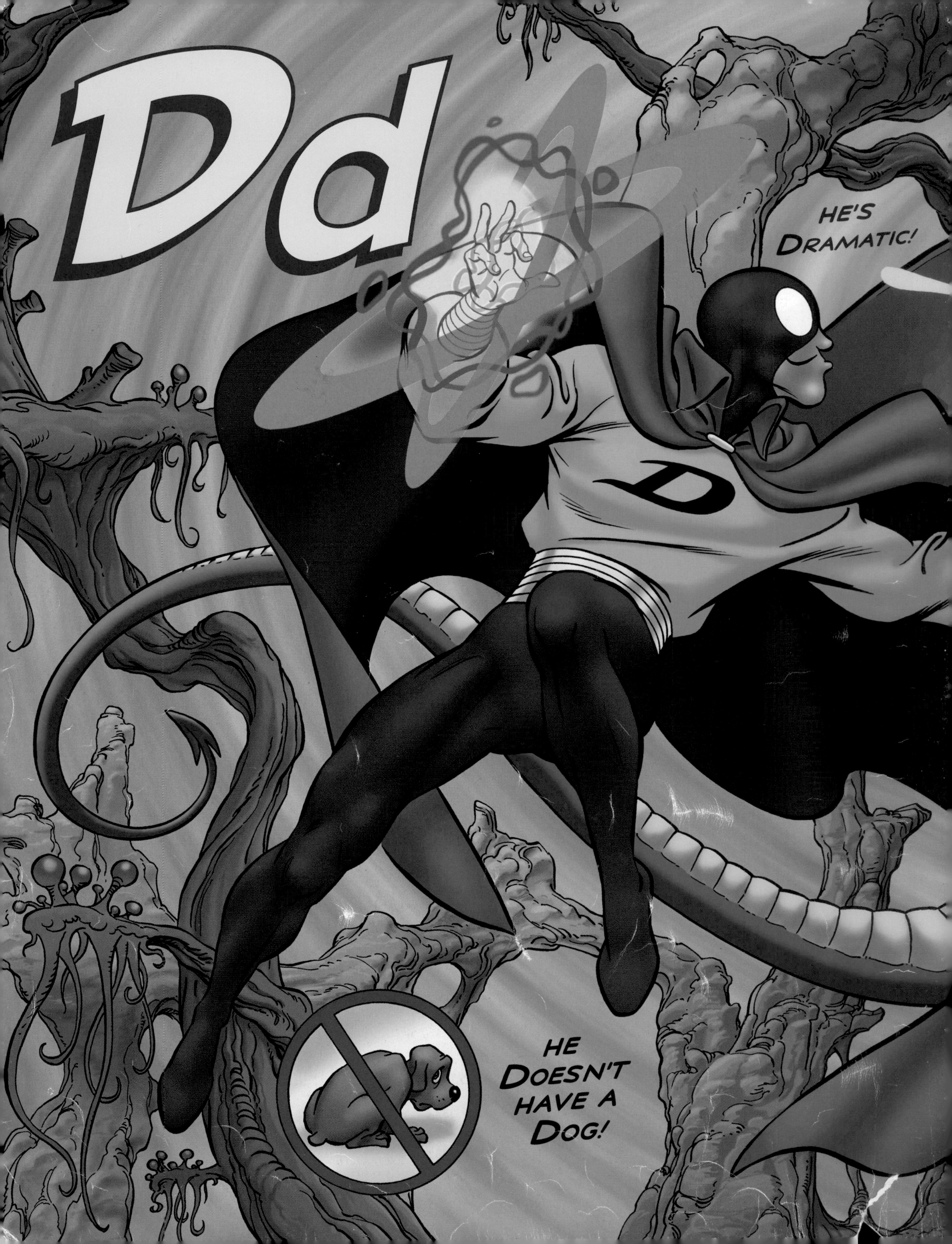

Dd
HE'S DRAMATIC!
HE DOESN'T HAVE A DOG!

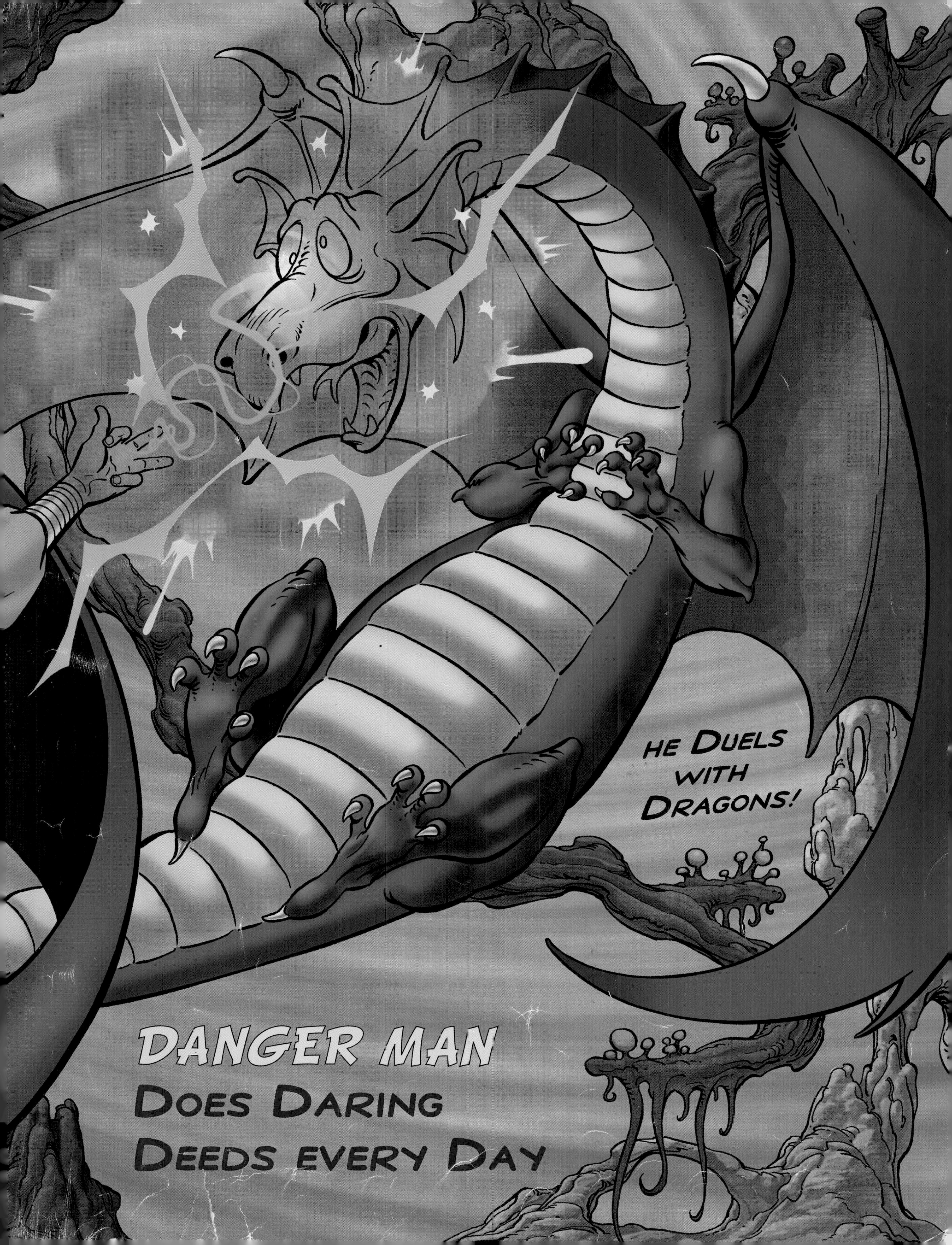
HE DUELS WITH DRAGONS!
DANGER MAN
Does Daring
Deeds every Day

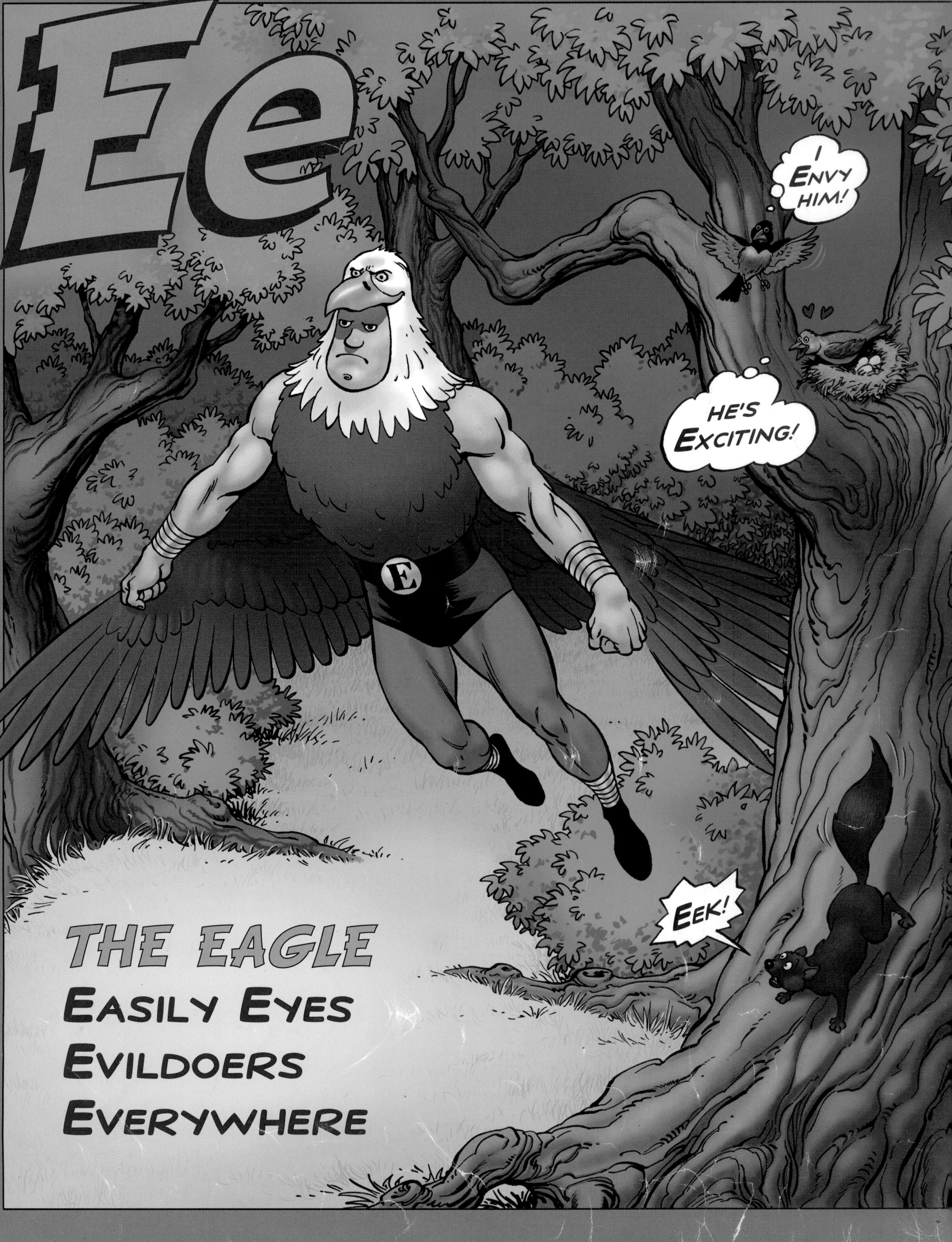

Ee
I ENVY HIM!
HE'S EXCITING!
EEK!
THE EAGLE
EASILY EYES
EVILDOERS
EVERYWHERE

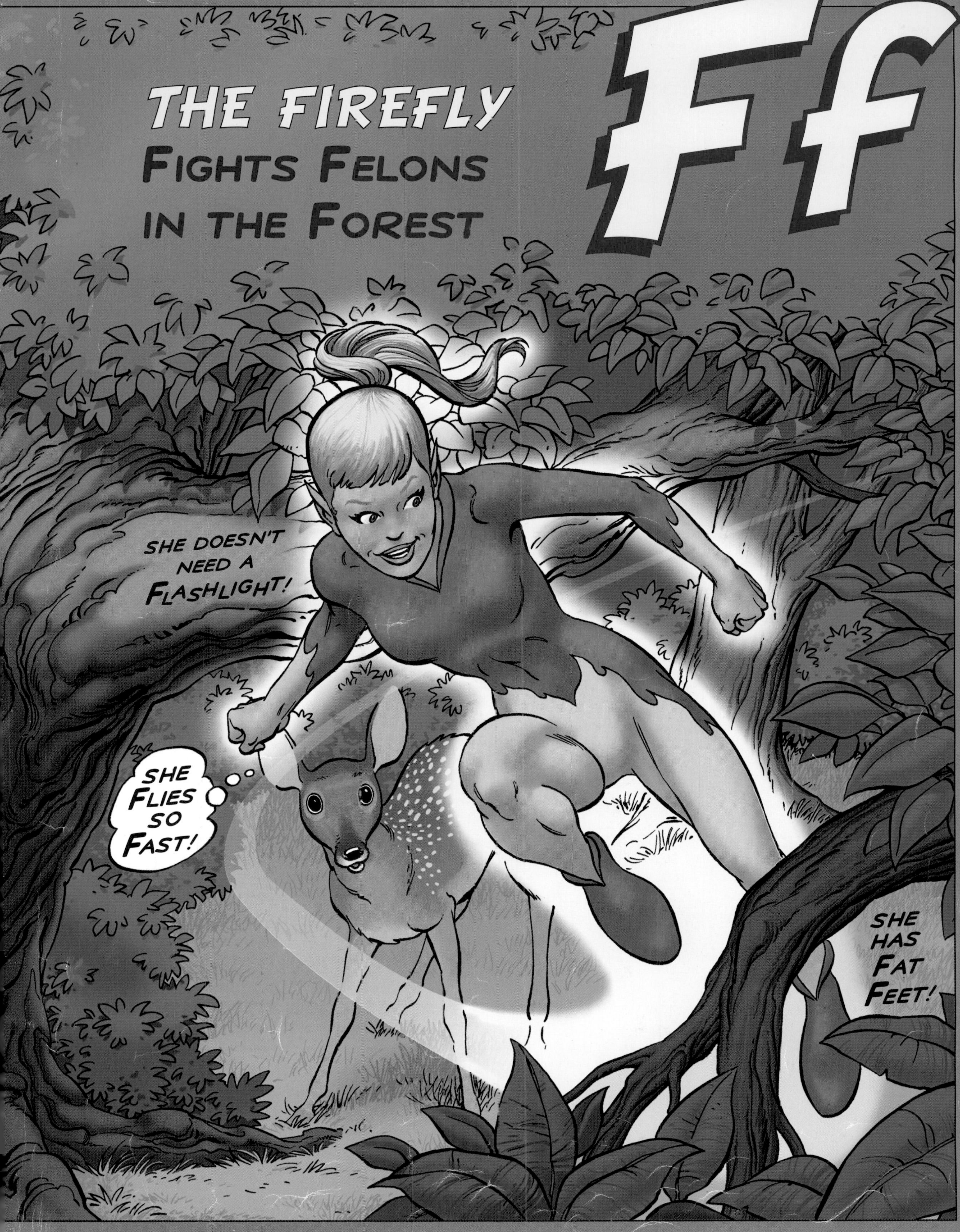
Ff
THE FIREFLY
FIGHTS FELONS IN THE FOREST
SHE DOESN'T NEED A FLASHLIGHT!
SHE FLIES SO FAST!
SHE HAS FAT FEET!

Gg

GOO GIRL SHOOTS GREAT GOBS OF GOO AT GANGSTERS

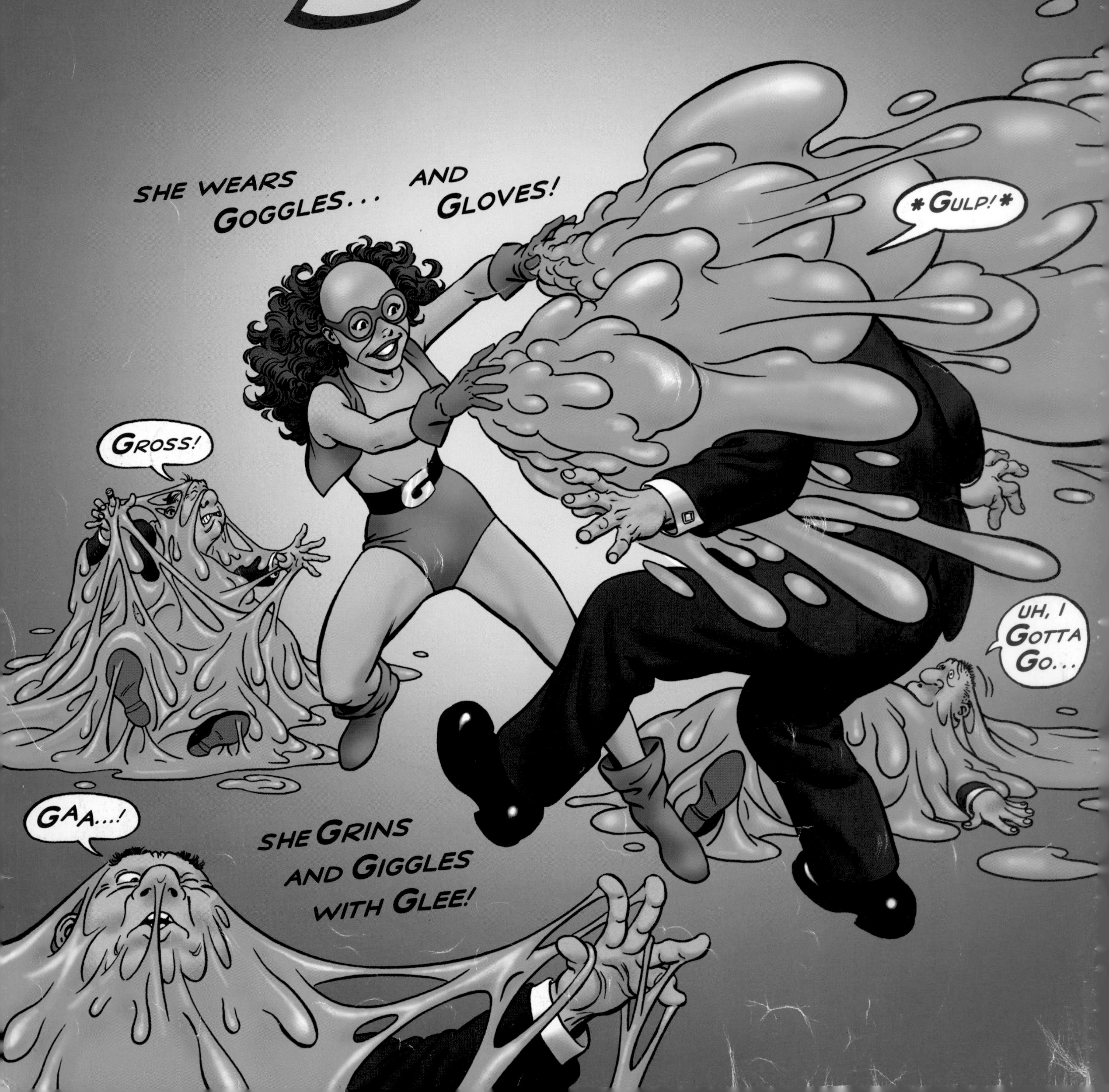
SHE WEARS GOGGLES...
AND GLOVES!
GULP!
GROSS!
UH, I GOTTA GO...
GAA...!
SHE GRINS AND GIGGLES WITH GLEE!

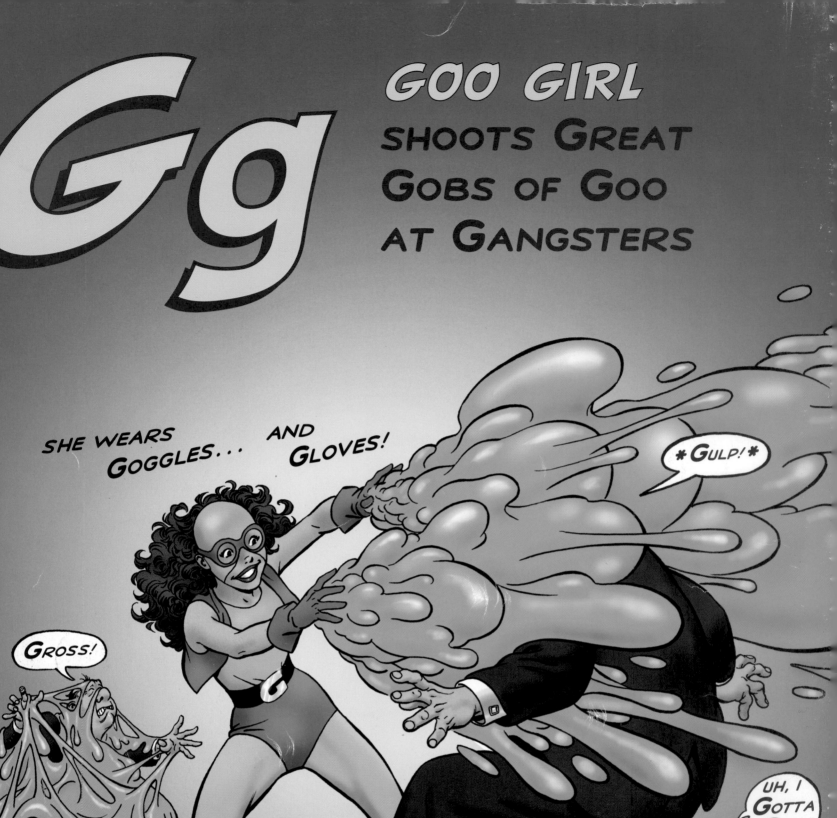

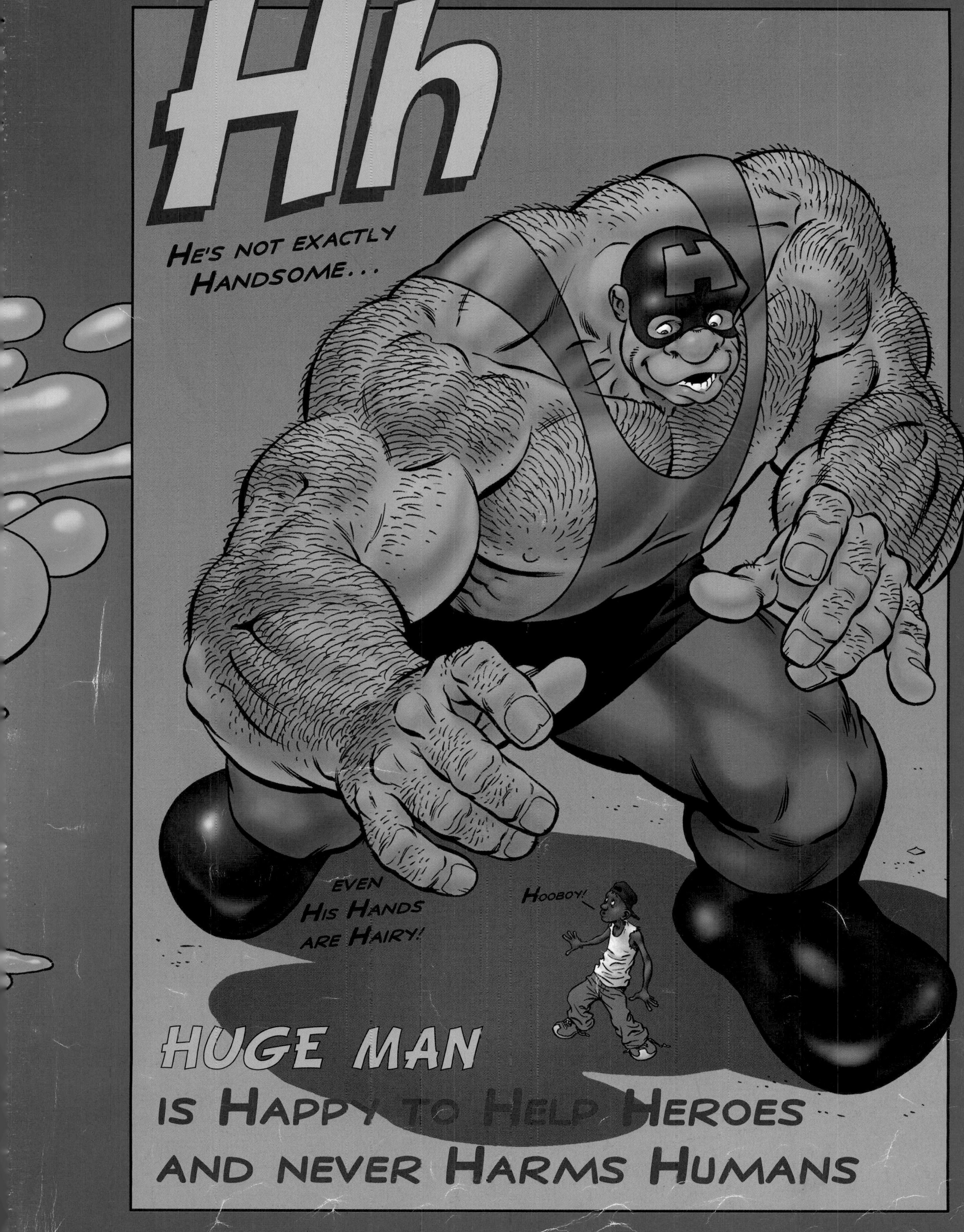
Hh
HE'S NOT EXACTLY HANDSOME...
EVEN HIS HANDS ARE HAIRY!
HOOBOY!
HUGE MAN
IS HAPPY TO HELP HEROES
AND NEVER HARMS HUMANS

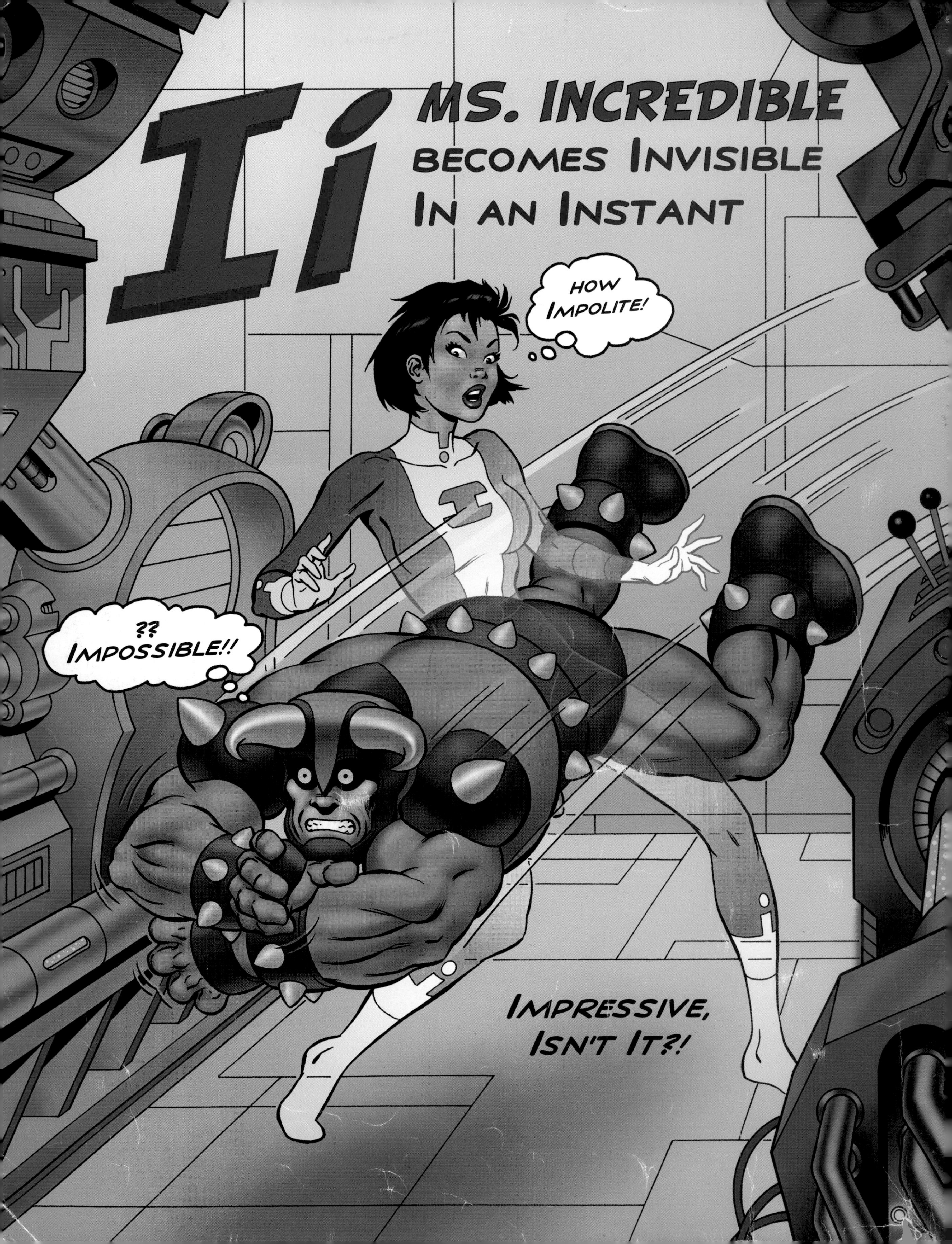
Ii
MS. INCREDIBLE
BECOMES INVISIBLE
IN AN INSTANT
HOW IMPOLITE!
?? IMPOSSIBLE!!
IMPRESSIVE, ISN'T IT?!

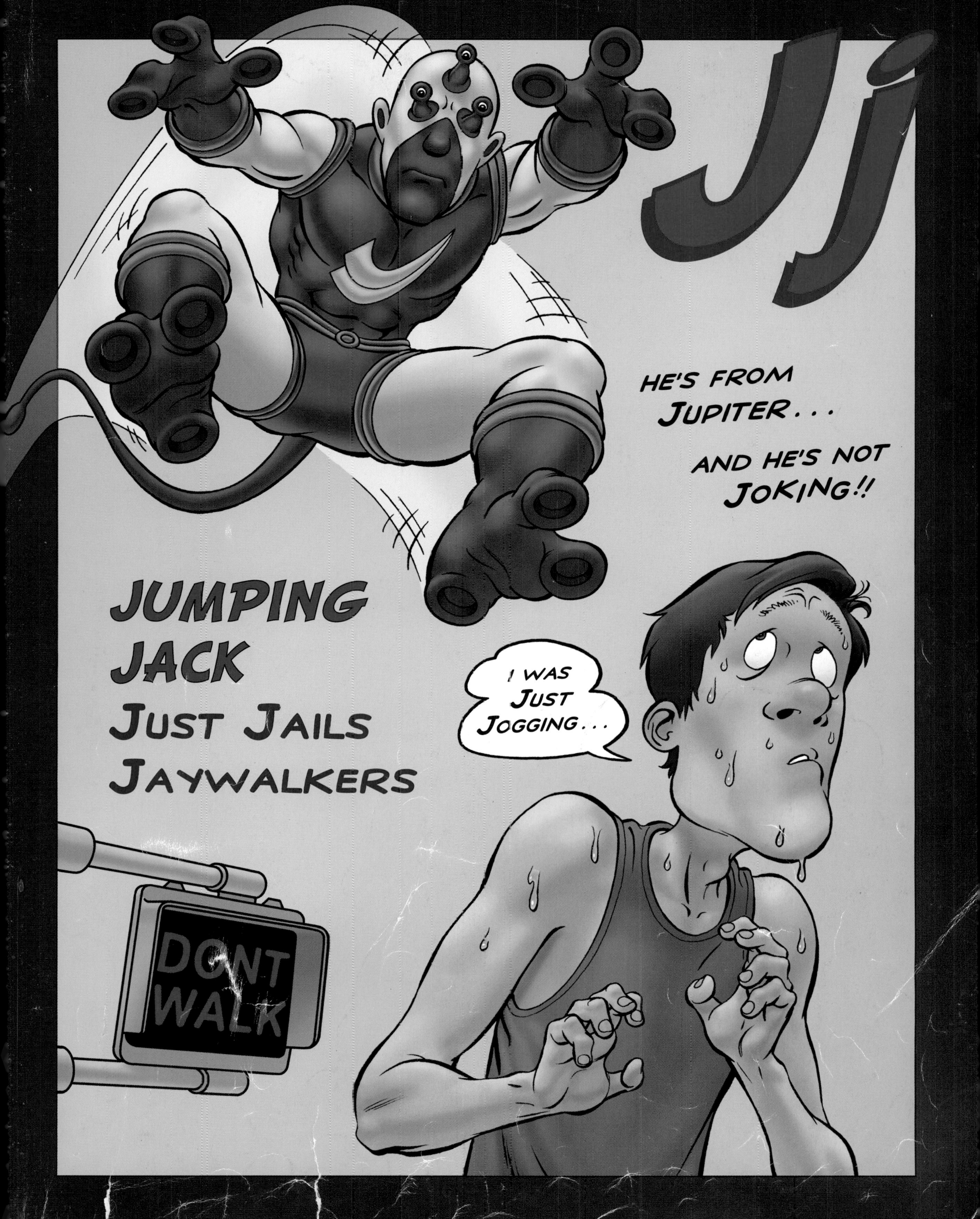
Jj
HE'S FROM JUPITER...
AND HE'S NOT JOKING!!
JUMPING JACK
JUST JAILS JAYWALKERS
I WAS JUST JOGGING...
DONT WALK

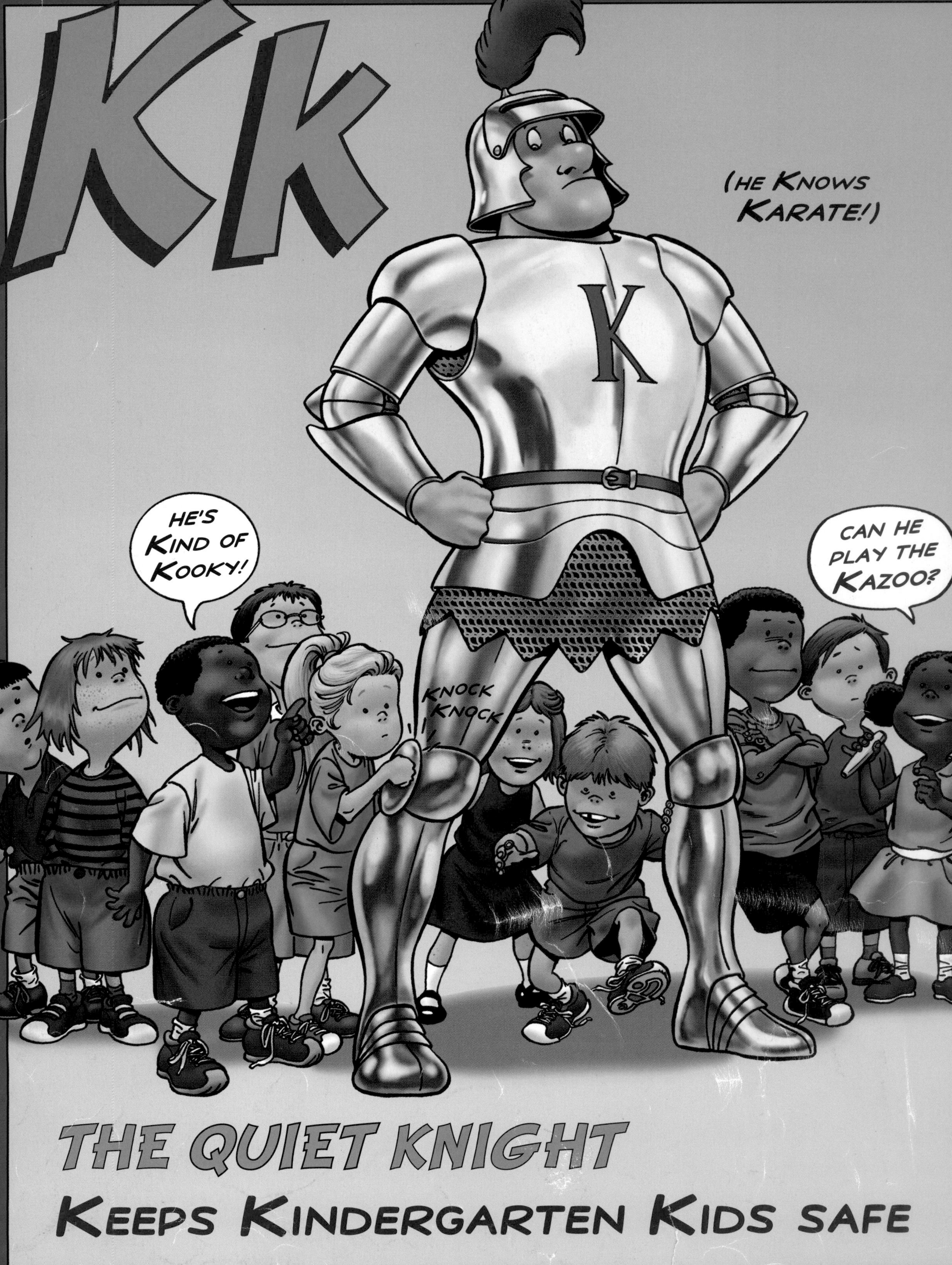
Kk
(HE KNOWS KARATE!)
K
HE'S KIND OF KOOKY!
CAN HE PLAY THE KAZOO?
KNOCK KNOCK
THE QUIET KNIGHT
KEEPS KINDERGARTEN KIDS SAFE

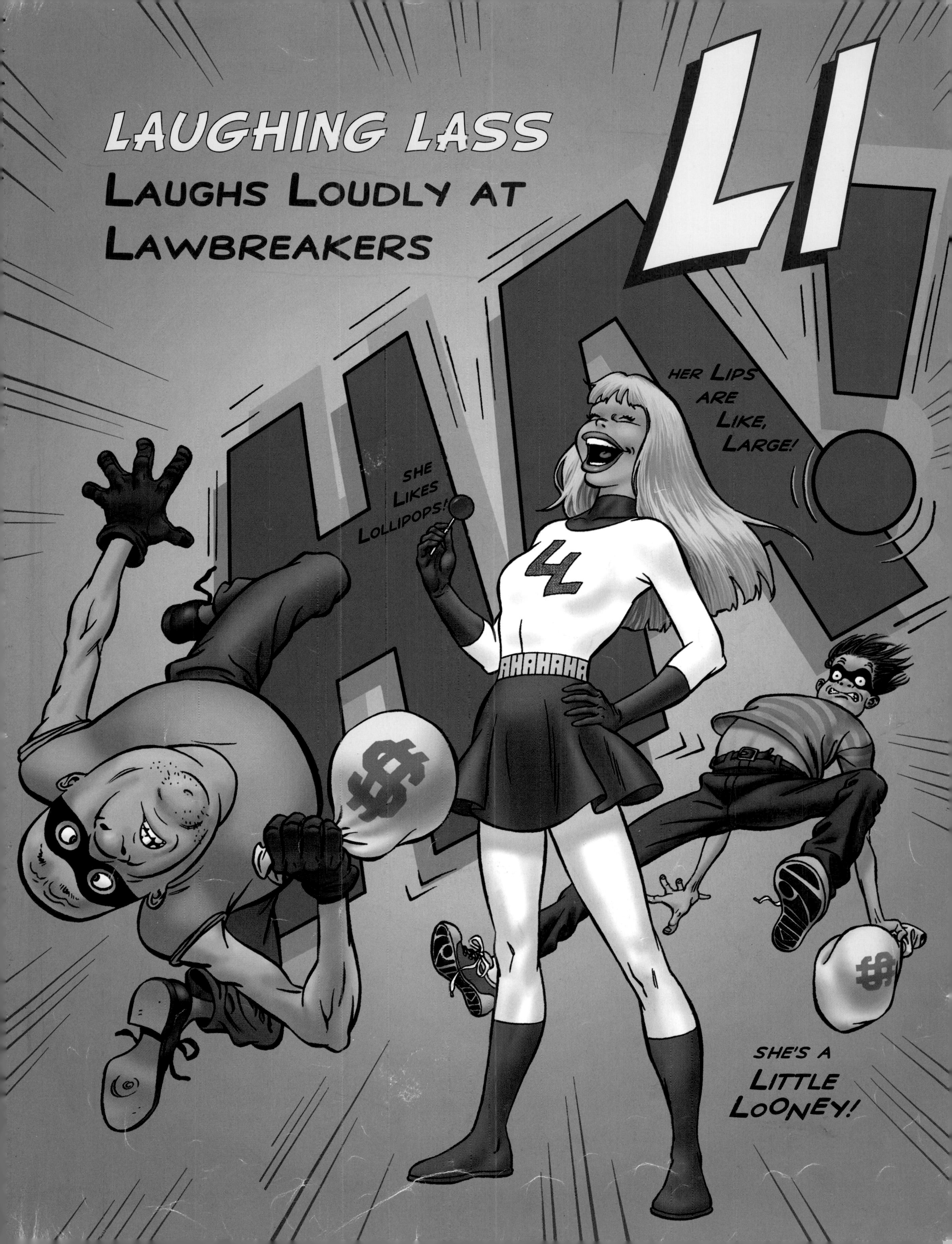

LAUGHING LASS
LAUGHS LOUDLY AT LAWBREAKERS
LL
HA!
HER LIPS ARE LIKE, LARGE!
SHE LIKES LOLLIPOPS!
L
AHAHAHAHA
SHE'S A LITTLE LOONEY!

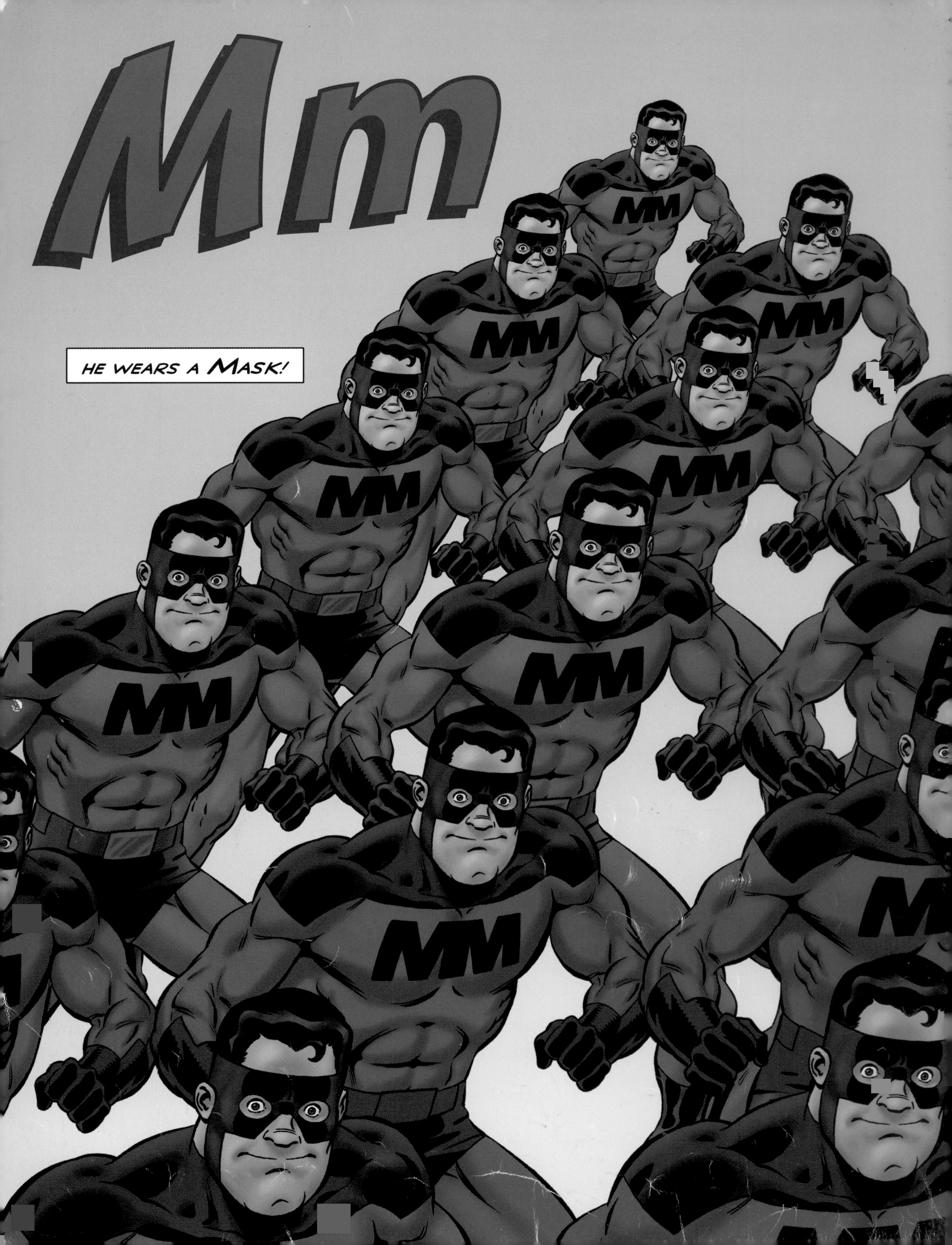
Mm
HE WEARS A MASK!
MM
MM
MM
MM
MM
MM
MM

MULTIPLYING MIKE BECOMES MANY MORE MEN IN MOMENTS

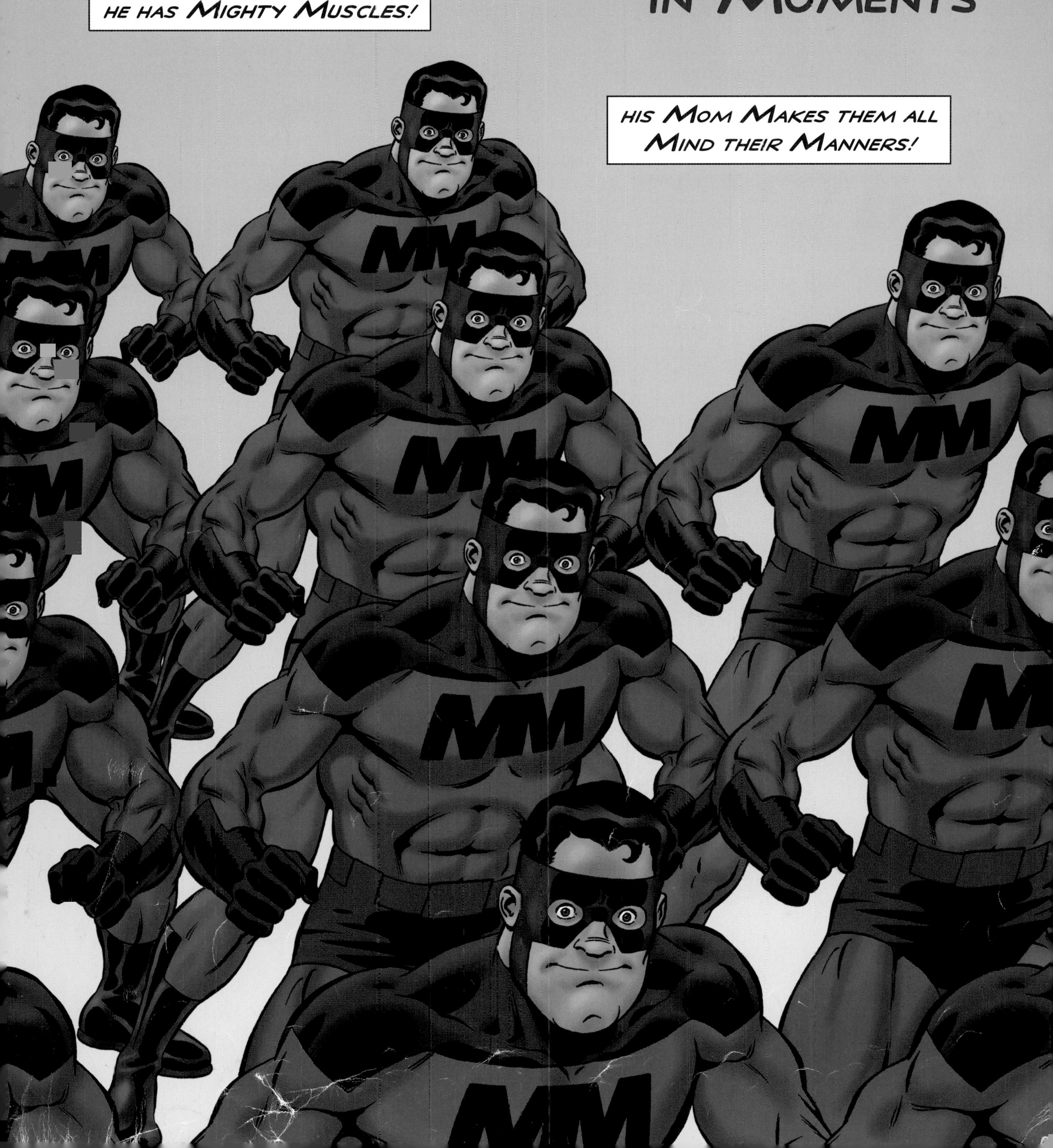
HE HAS MIGHTY MUSCLES!
HIS MOM MAKES THEM ALL MIND THEIR MANNERS!

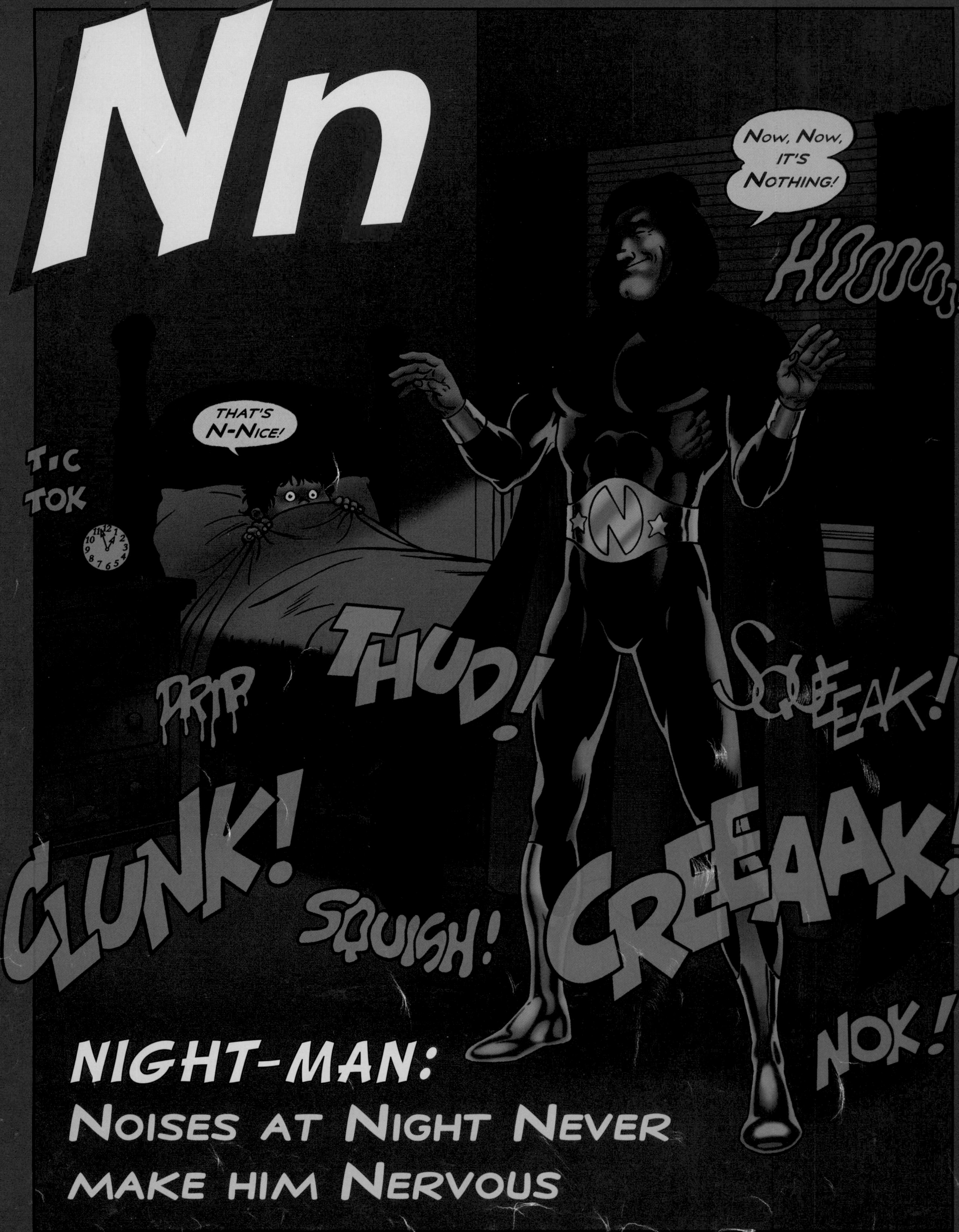Nn
Now, Now, it's Nothing!
HOOOOOOO
That's N-Nice!
Tic Tok
Drip
Thud!
Squeeak!
Clunk!
Squish!
Creeaak!
Nok!
NIGHT-MAN:
Noises at Night Never make him Nervous

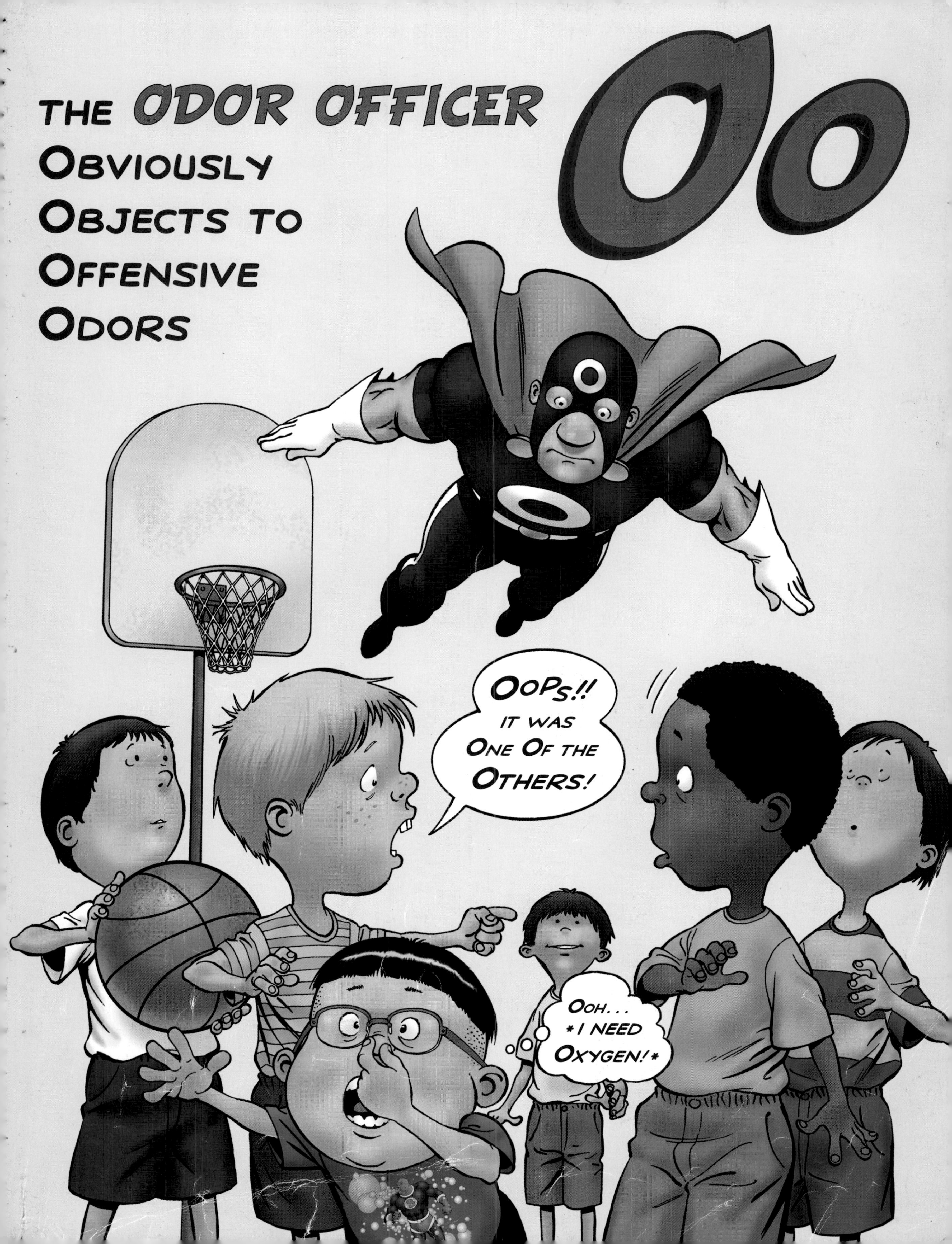
THE ODOR OFFICER
Oo
OBVIOUSLY OBJECTS TO OFFENSIVE ODORS
OOPS!! IT WAS ONE OF THE OTHERS!
OOH... *I NEED OXYGEN!*

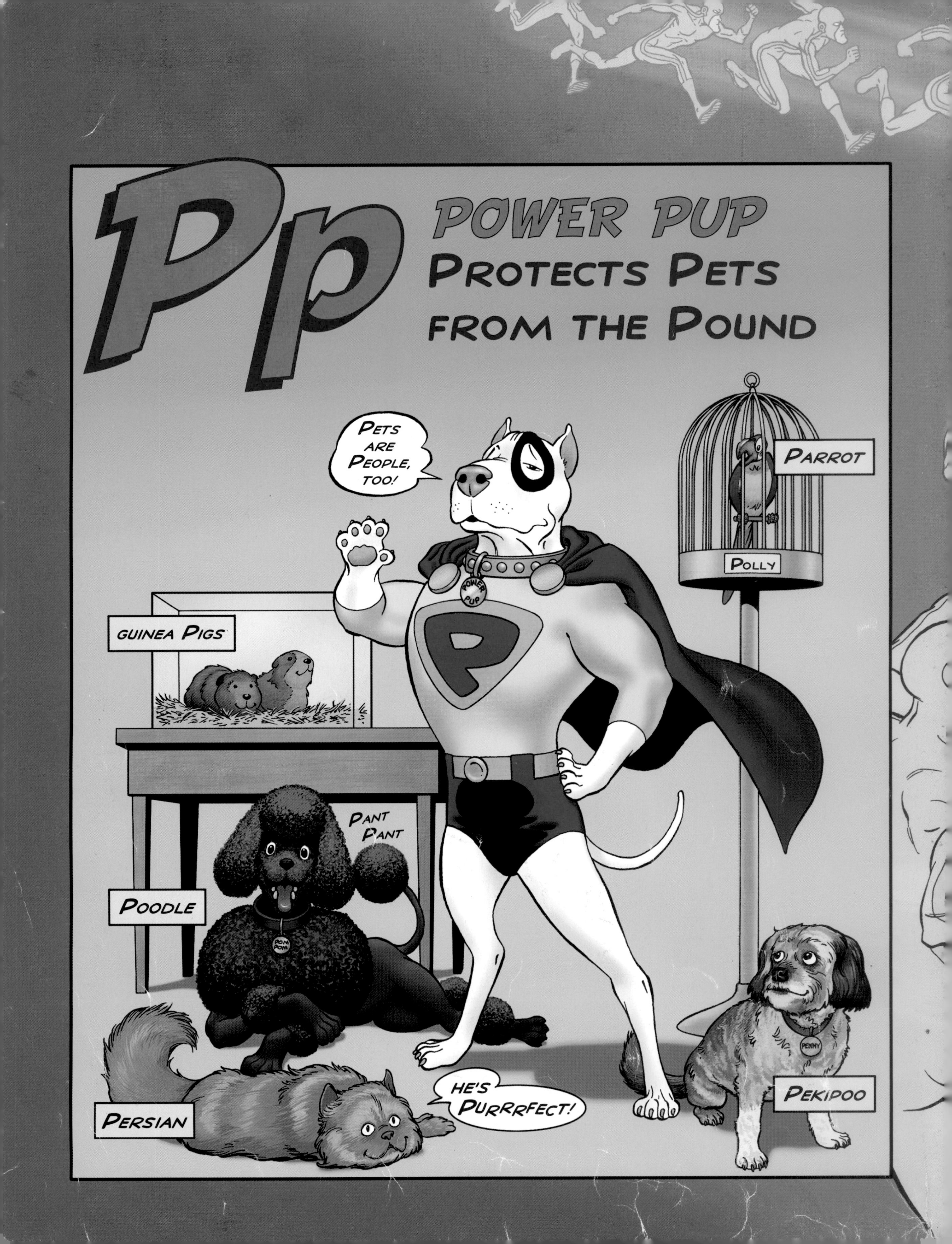
Pp
POWER PUP
PROTECTS PETS
FROM THE POUND
PETS ARE PEOPLE, TOO!
PARROT
POLLY
POWER PUP
GUINEA PIGS
PANT PANT
POODLE
POM POM
PENNY
HE'S PURRRFECT!
PEKIPOO
PERSIAN

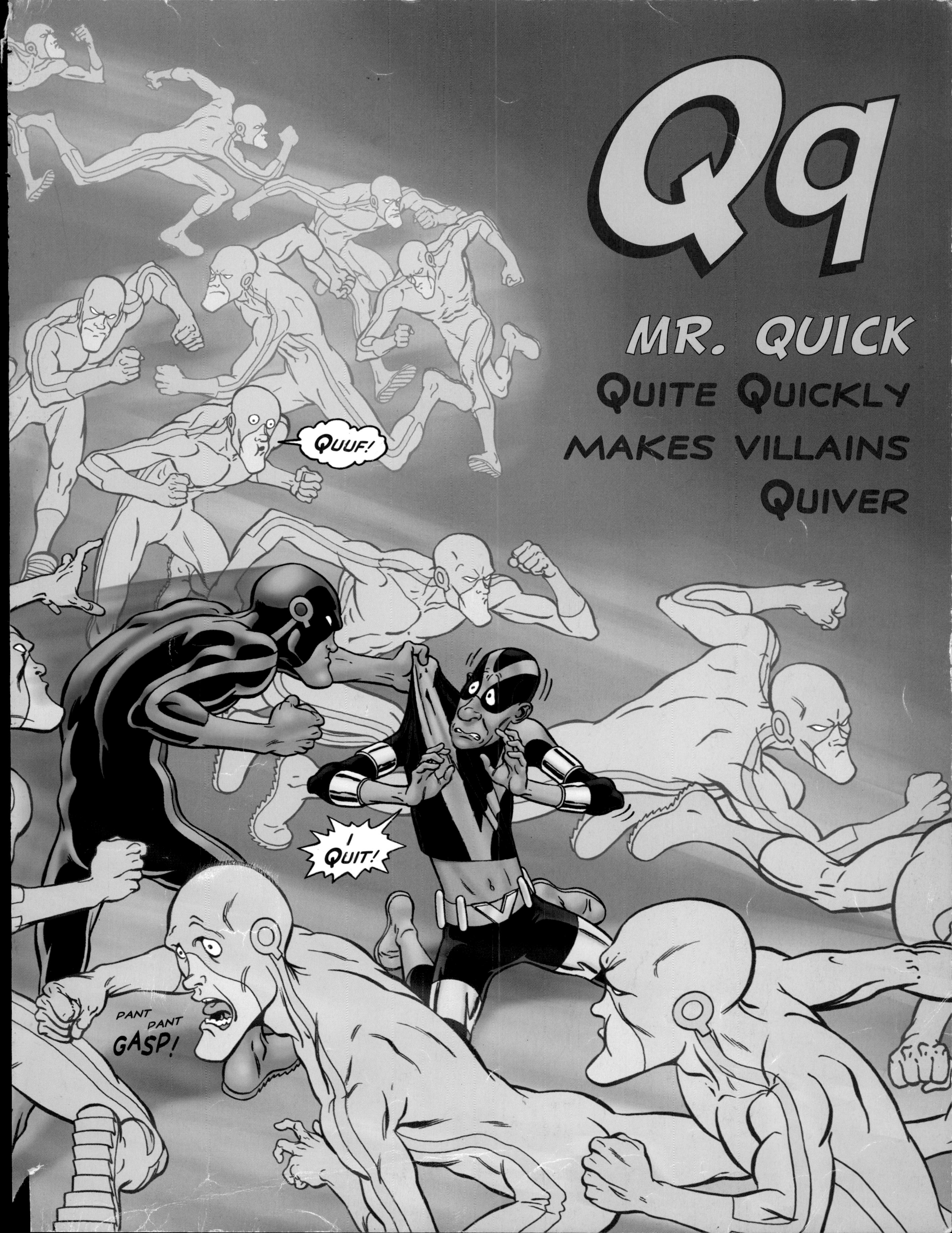

Qq
MR. QUICK
Quite Quickly
makes villains
Quiver
QUUF!
I QUIT!
PANT PANT
GASP!

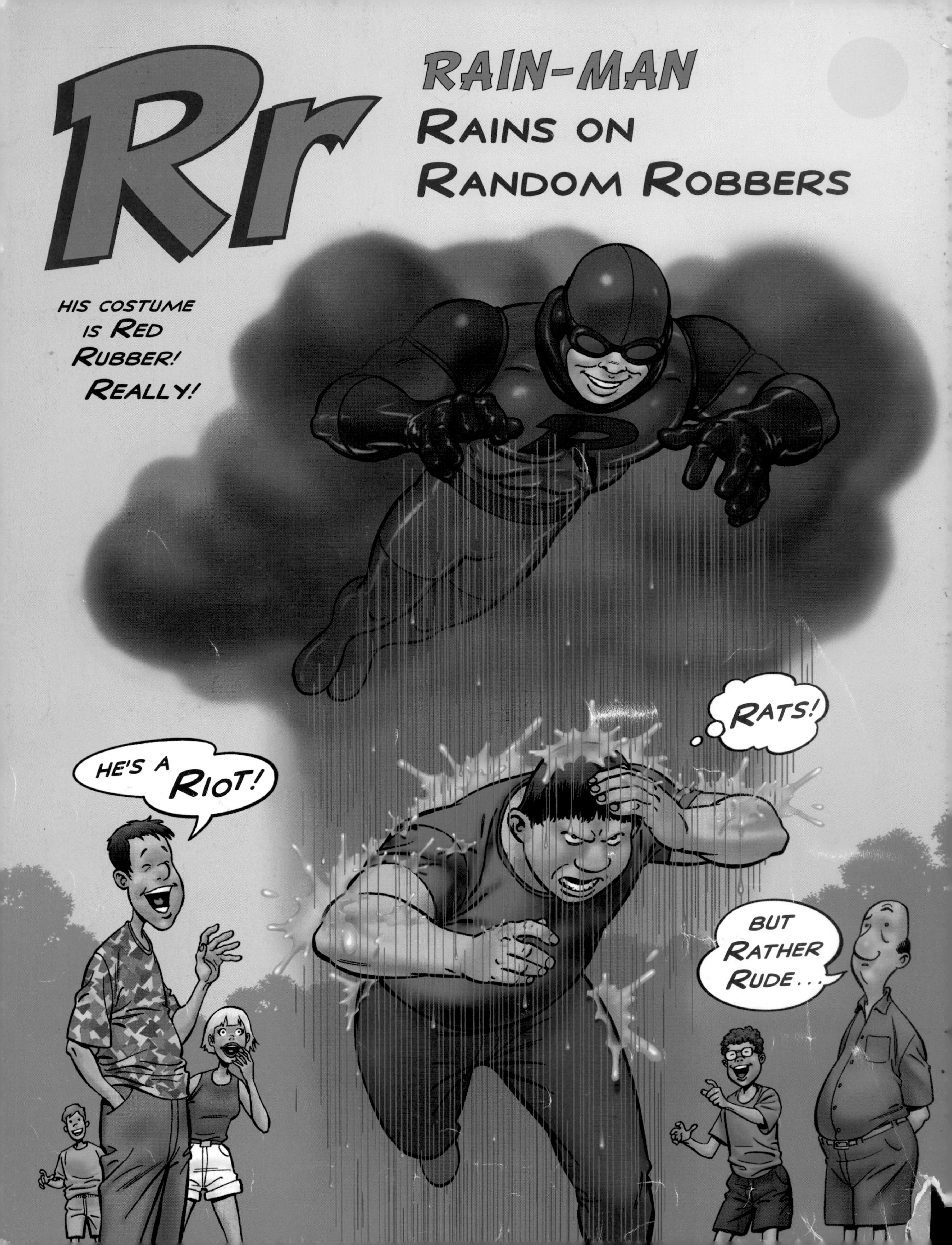
Rr
RAIN-MAN
RAINS ON
RANDOM ROBBERS
HIS COSTUME IS RED RUBBER! REALLY!
RATS!
HE'S A RIOT!
BUT RATHER RUDE . . .

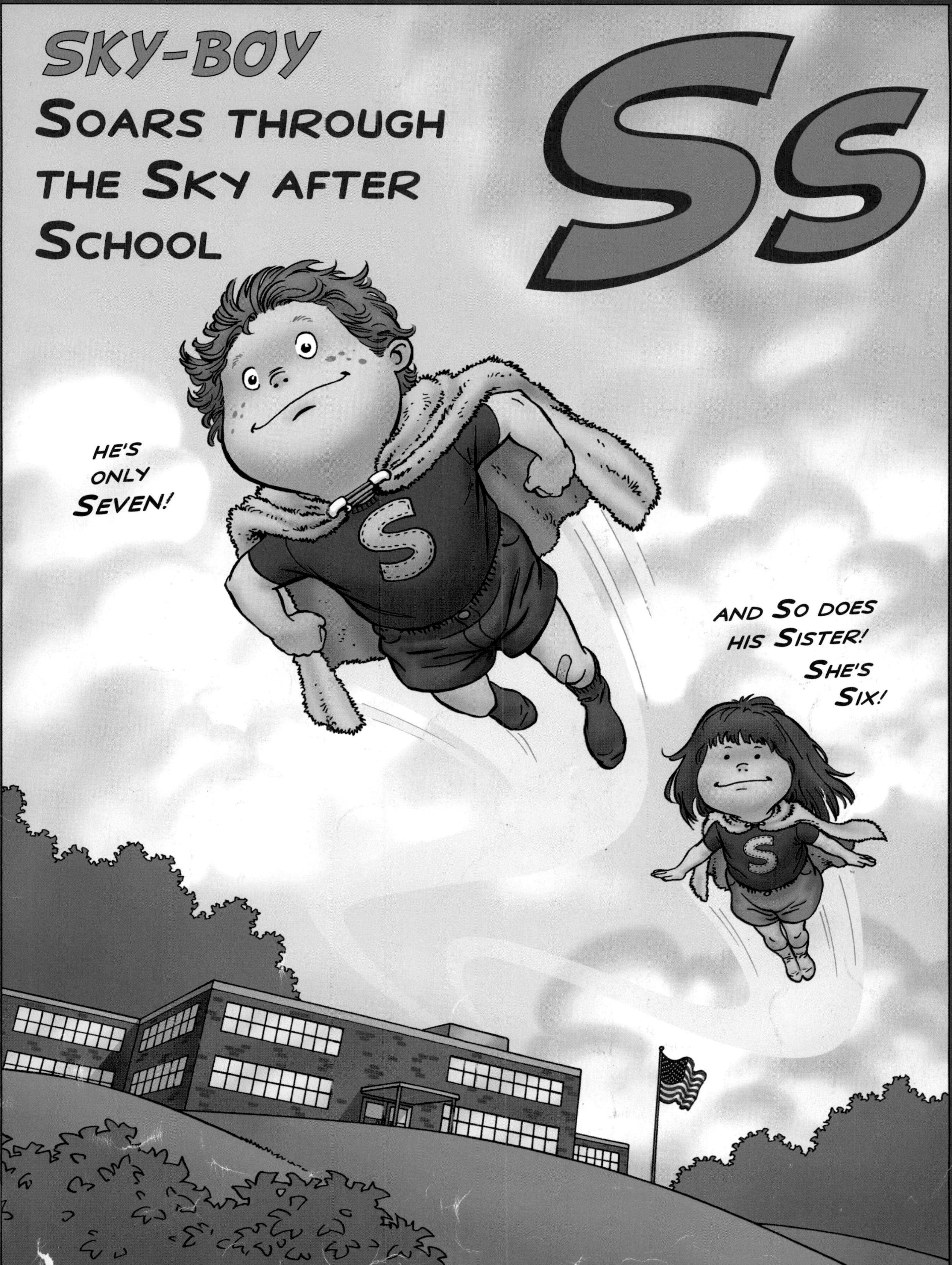
SKY-BOY
SOARS THROUGH THE SKY AFTER SCHOOL
Ss
HE'S ONLY SEVEN!
AND SO DOES HIS SISTER!
SHE'S SIX!

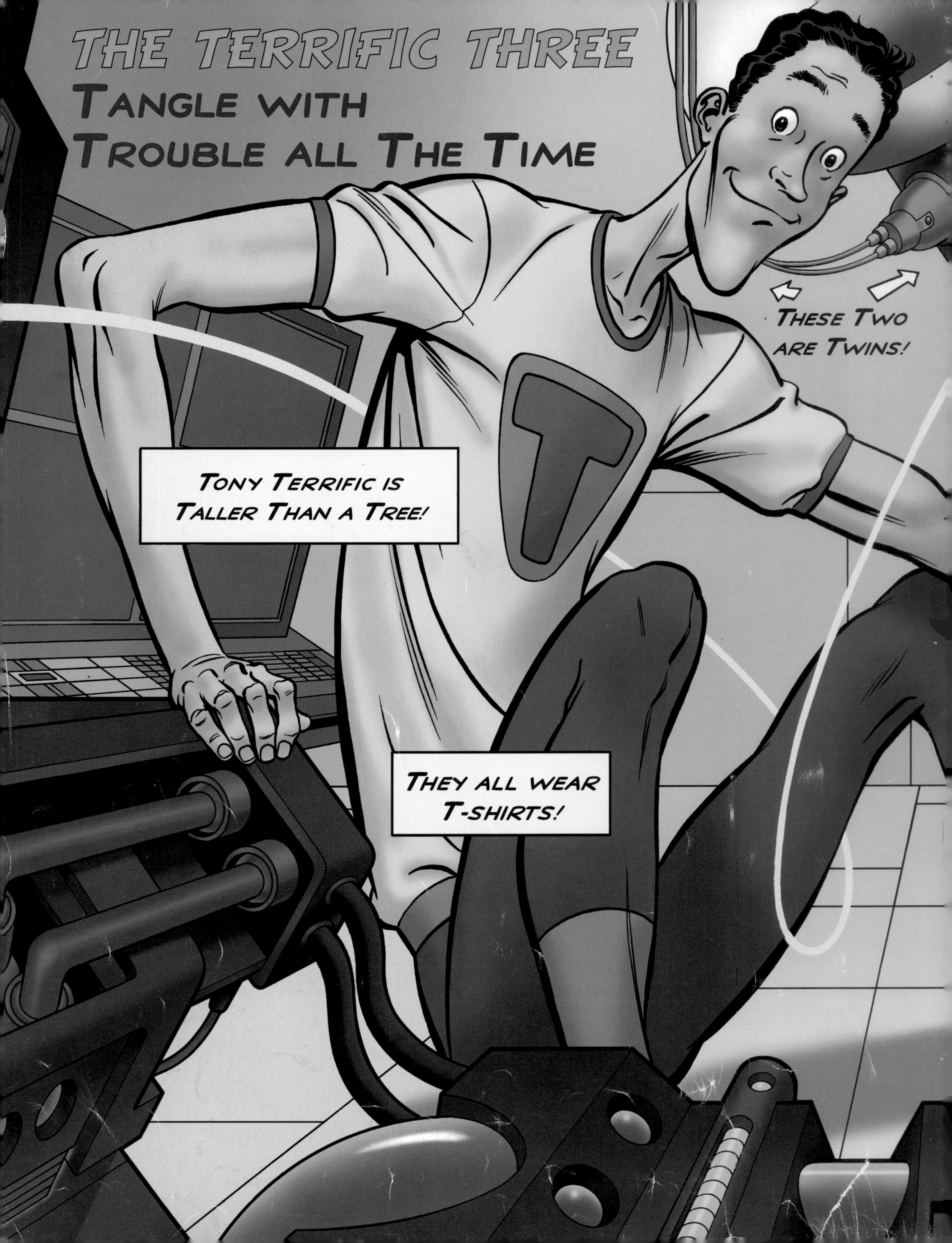
THE TERRIFIC THREE
TANGLE WITH
TROUBLE ALL THE TIME
THESE TWO ARE TWINS!
TONY TERRIFIC IS TALLER THAN A TREE!
THEY ALL WEAR T-SHIRTS!

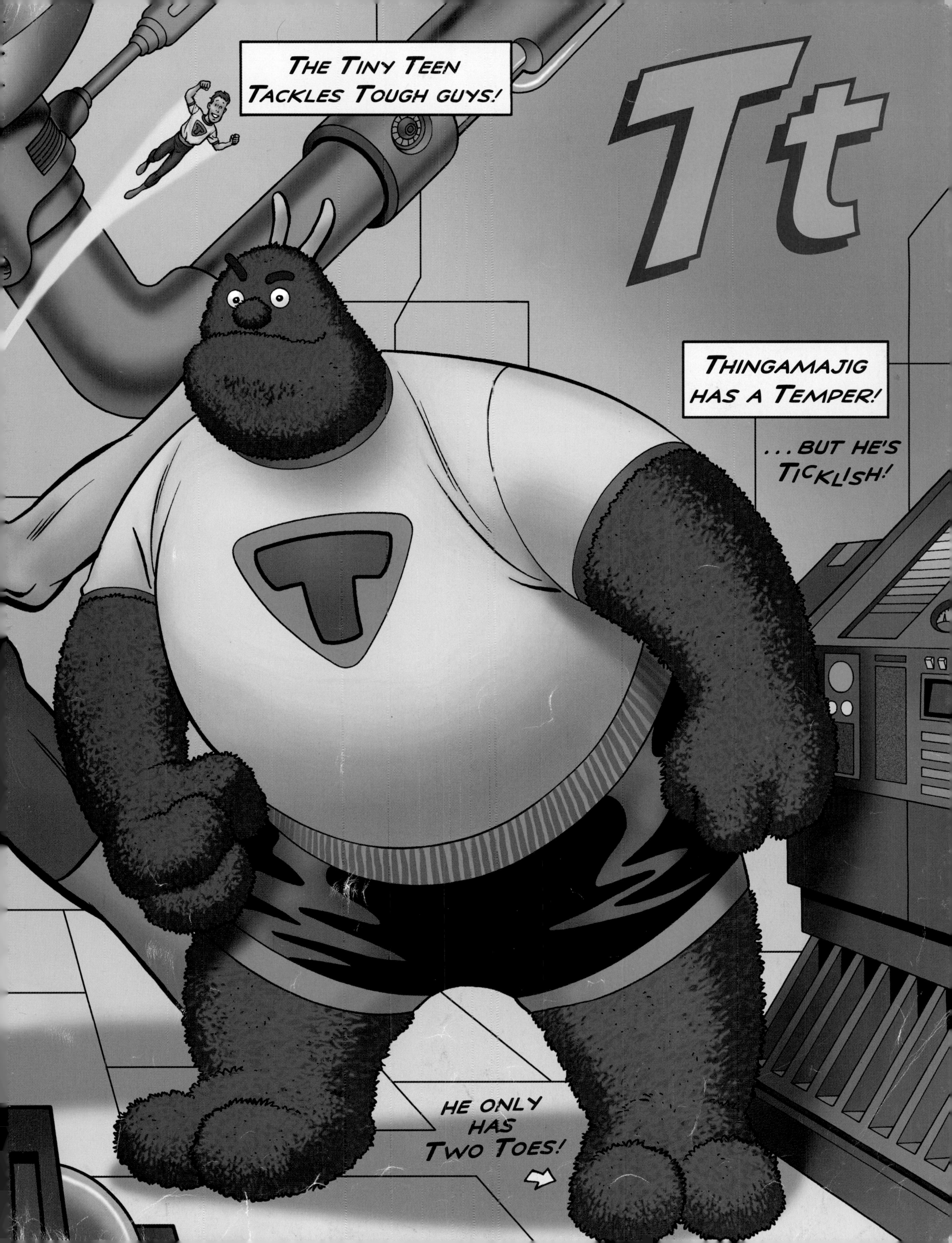
Tt
THE TINY TEEN TACKLES TOUGH GUYS!
THINGAMAJIG HAS A TEMPER!
...BUT HE'S TICKLISH!
HE ONLY HAS TWO TOES!

Uu

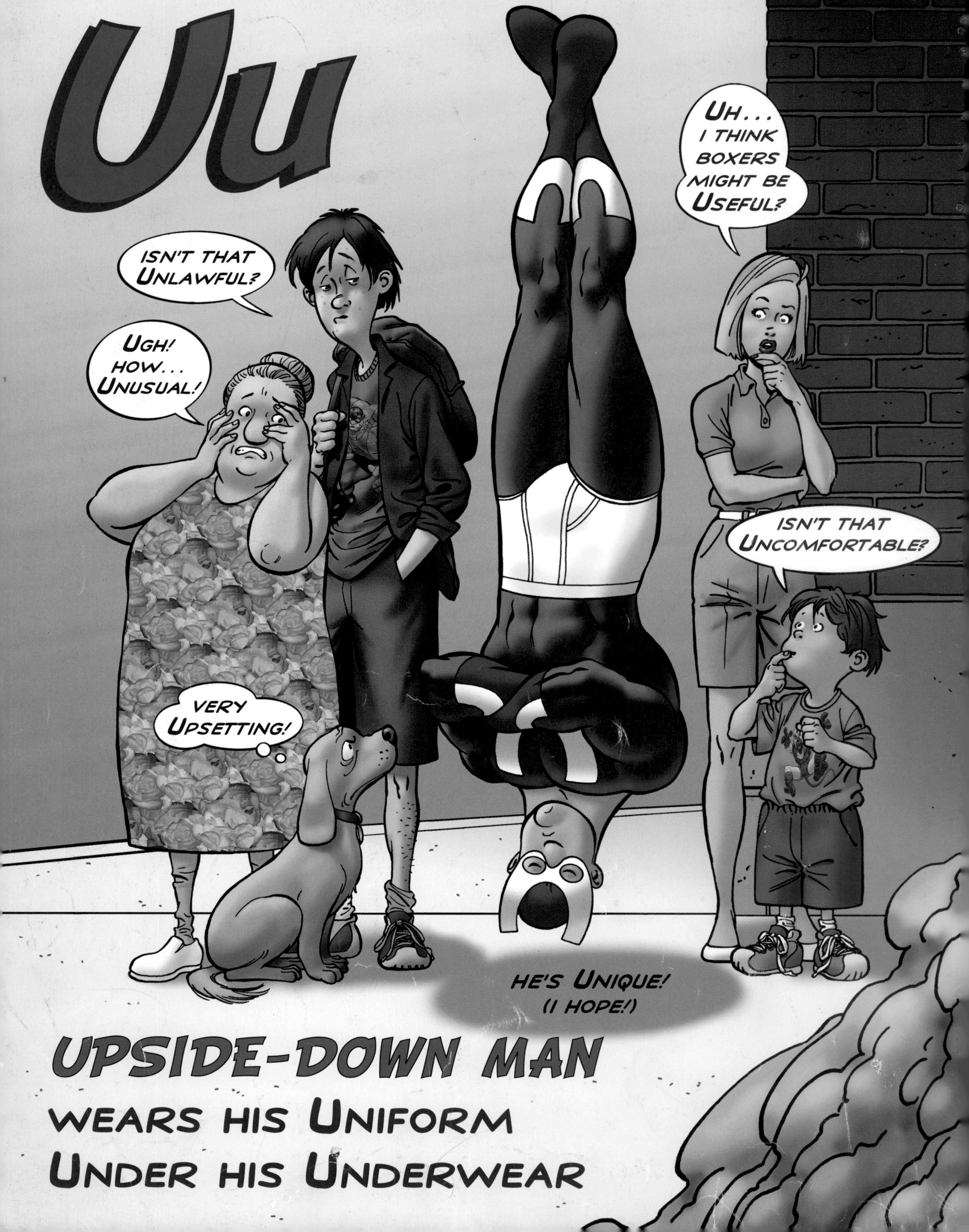
UH... I THINK BOXERS MIGHT BE USEFUL?
ISN'T THAT UNLAWFUL?
UGH! HOW... UNUSUAL!
ISN'T THAT UNCOMFORTABLE?
VERY UPSETTING!
HE'S UNIQUE! (I HOPE!)

UPSIDE-DOWN MAN

WEARS HIS UNIFORM
UNDER HIS UNDERWEAR

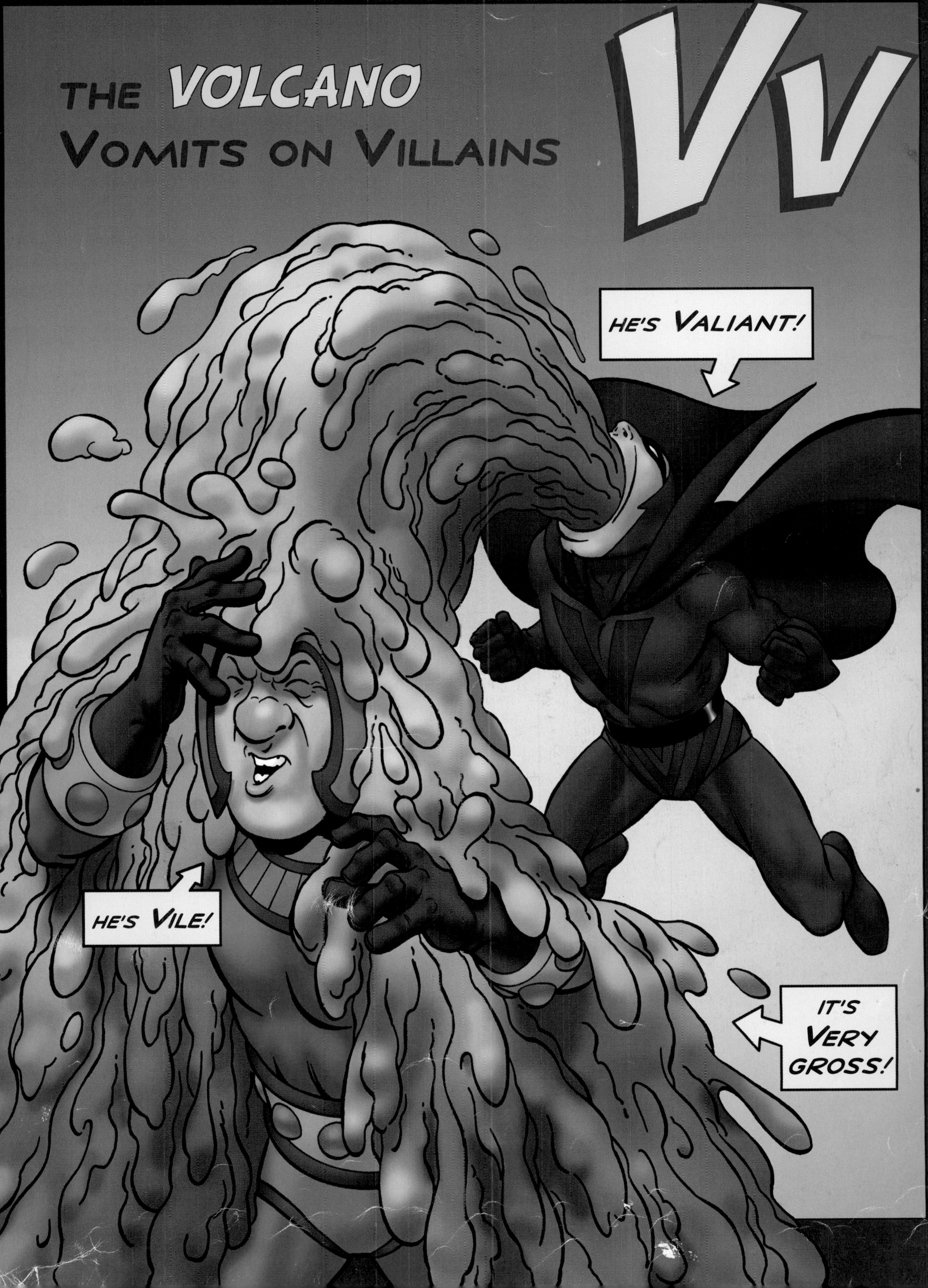
THE VOLCANO
VOMITS ON VILLAINS
Vv
HE'S VALIANT!
HE'S VILE!
IT'S VERY GROSS!

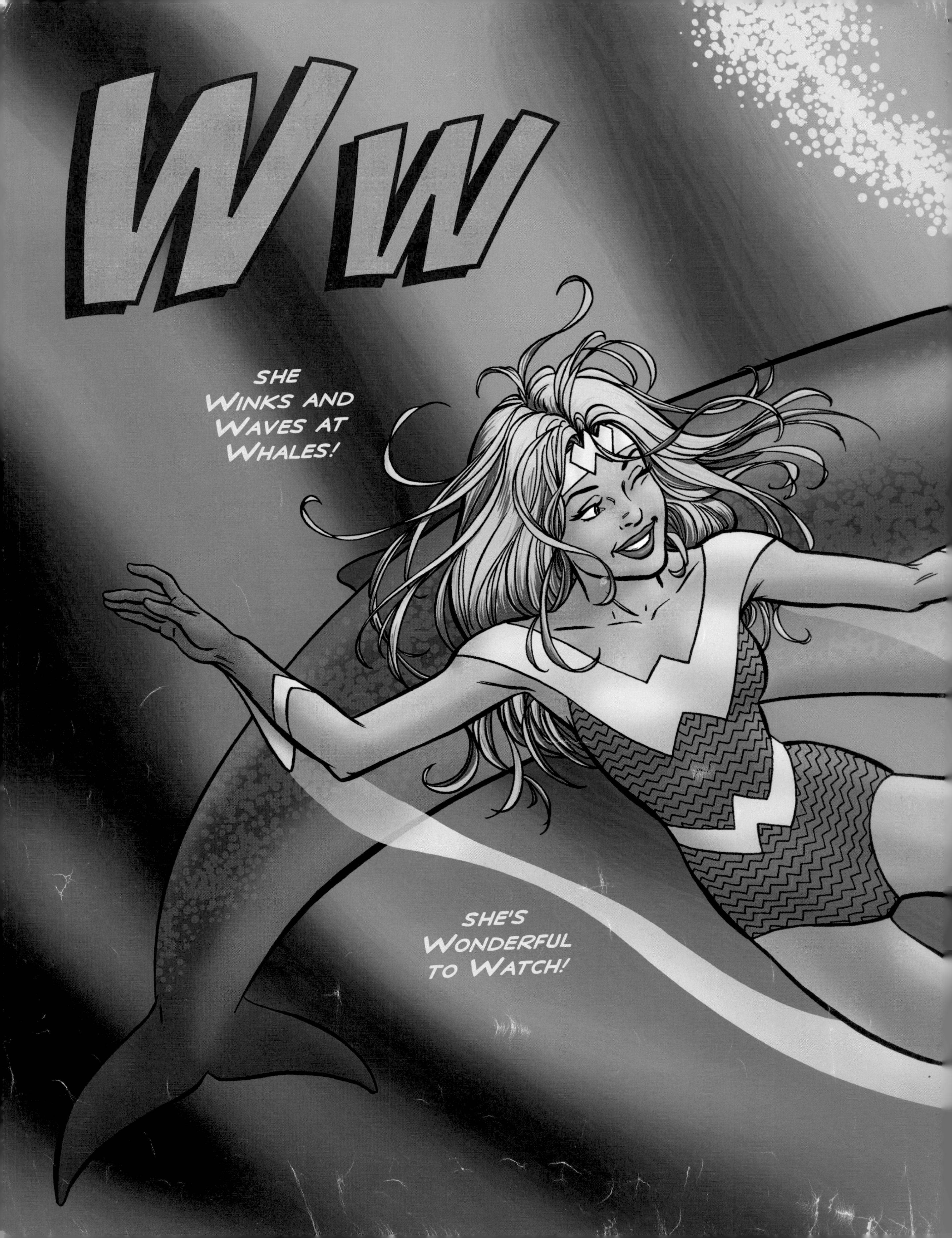
Ww
SHE WINKS AND WAVES AT WHALES!
SHE'S WONDERFUL TO WATCH!

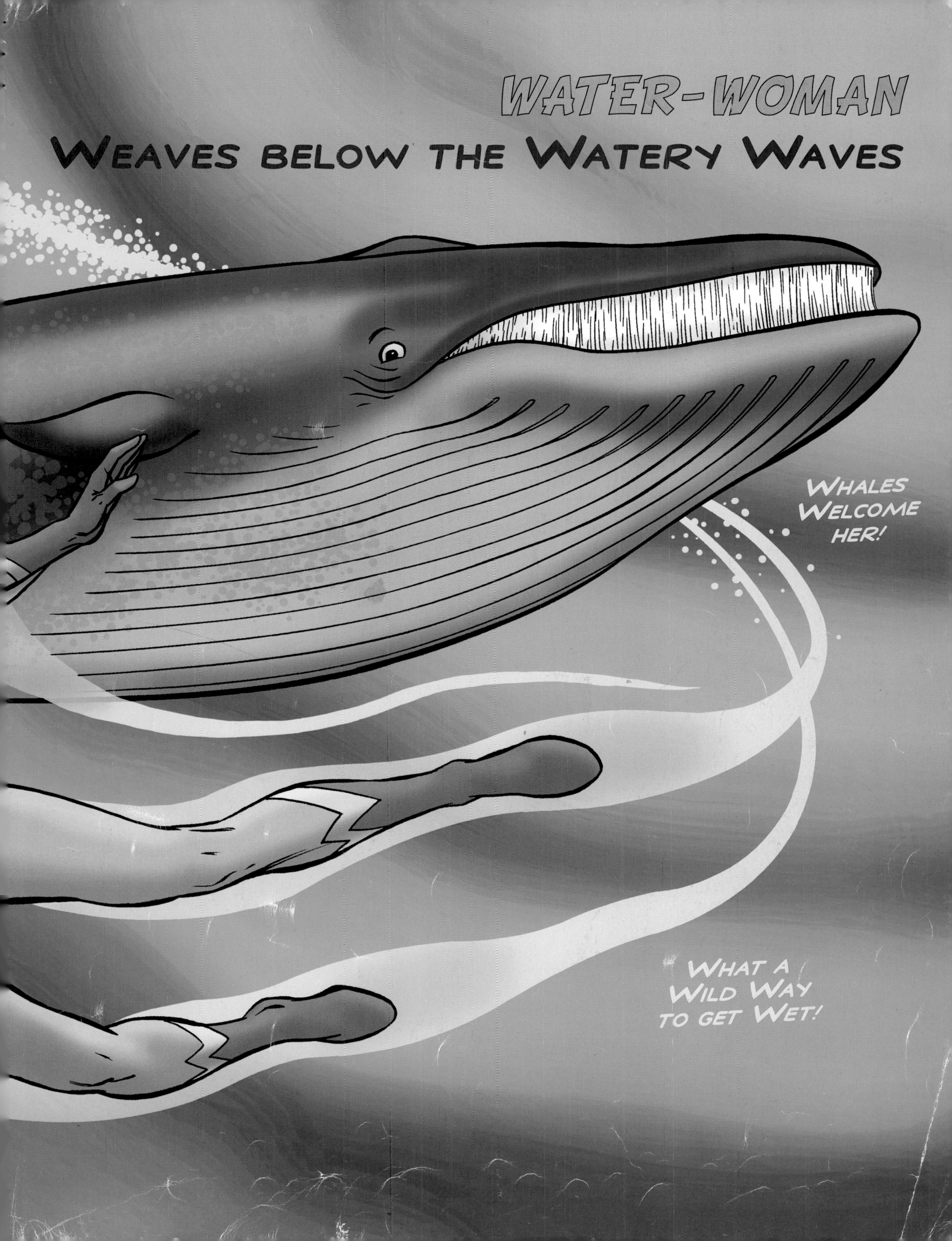
WATER-WOMAN
WEAVES BELOW THE WATERY WAVES
WHALES WELCOME HER!
WHAT A WILD WAY TO GET WET!

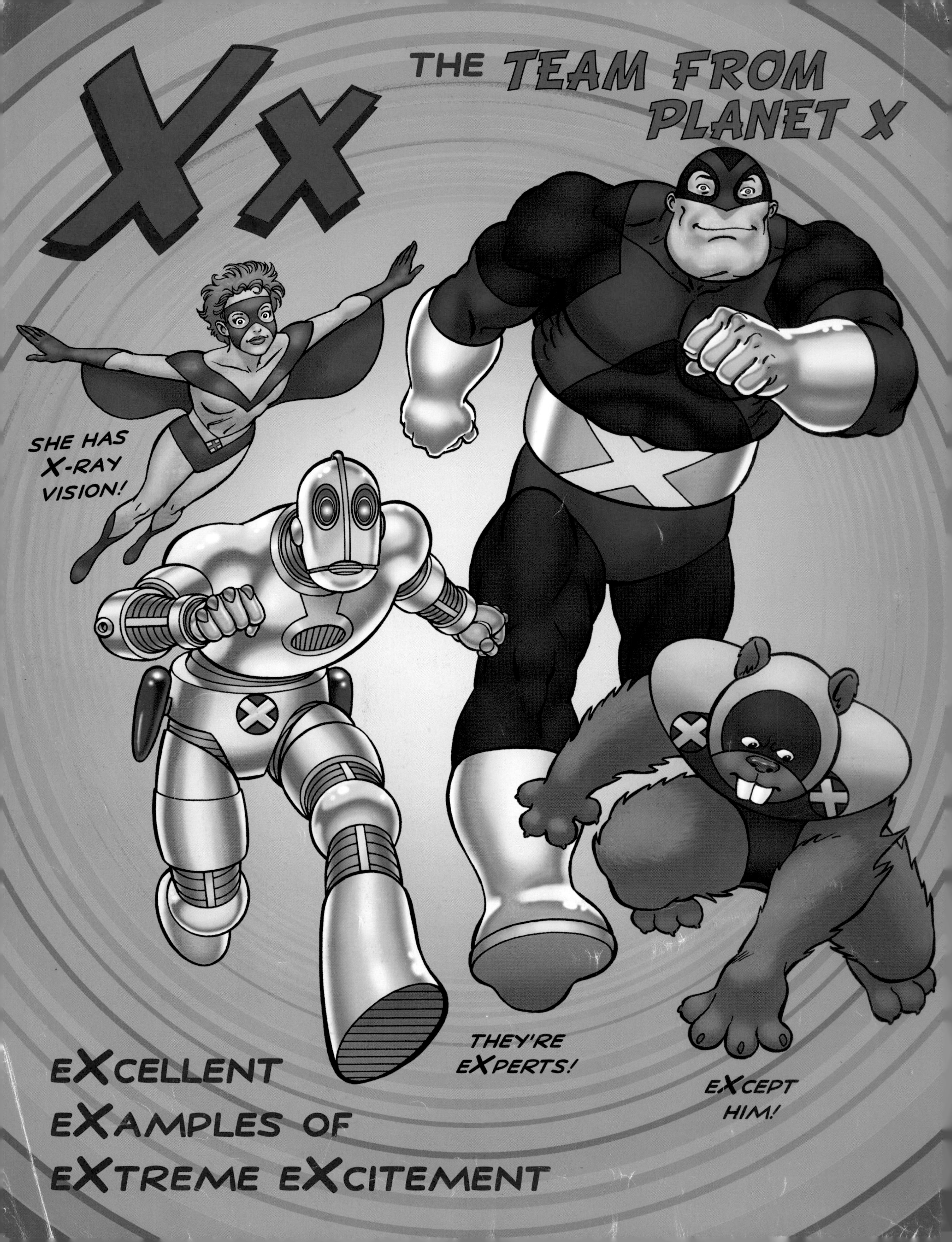
XX
THE TEAM FROM PLANET X
SHE HAS X-RAY VISION!
THEY'RE EXPERTS!
EXCEPT HIM!
EXCELLENT EXAMPLES OF EXTREME EXCITEMENT

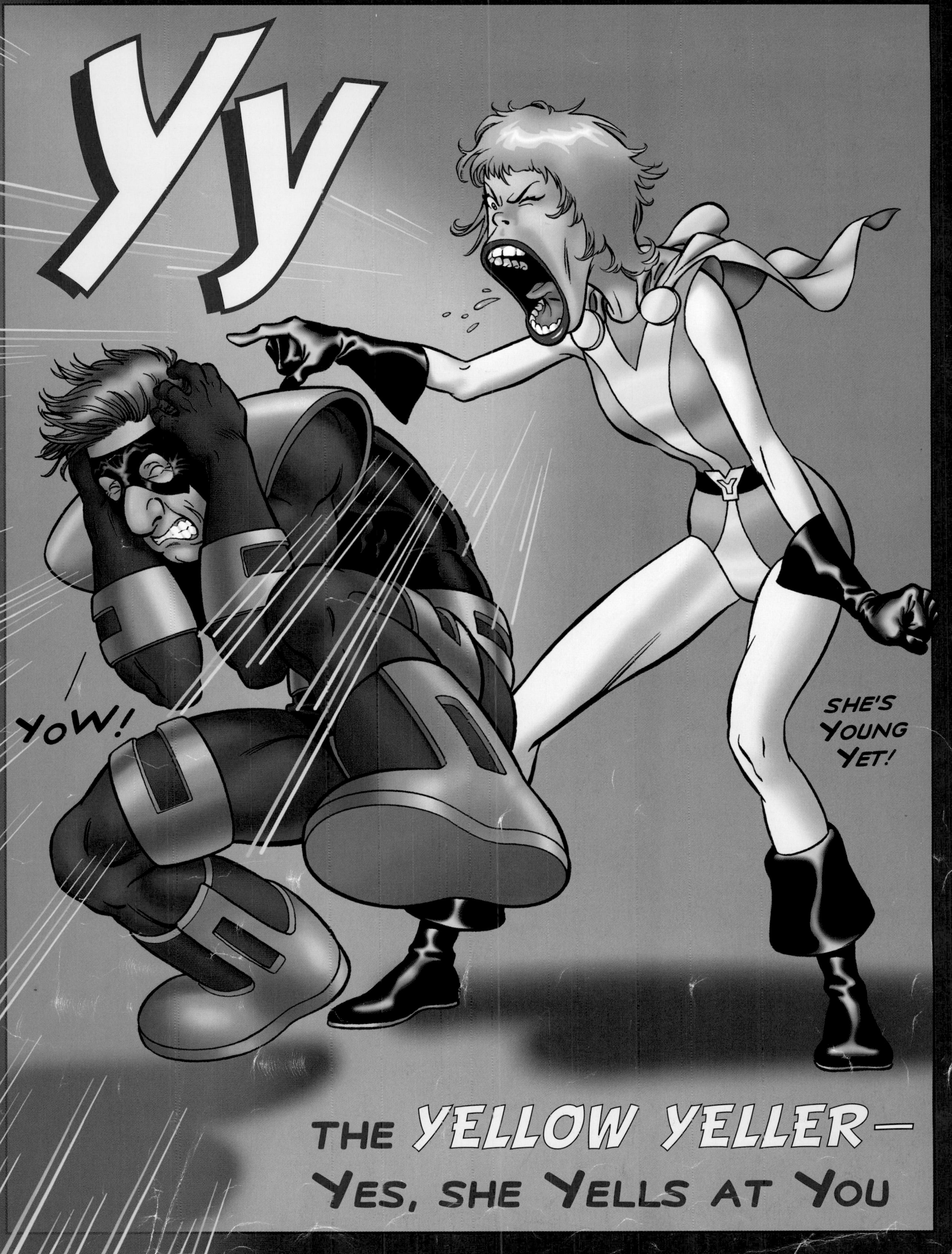
Yy
YOW!
SHE'S YOUNG YET!
THE YELLOW YELLER—
YES, SHE YELLS AT YOU

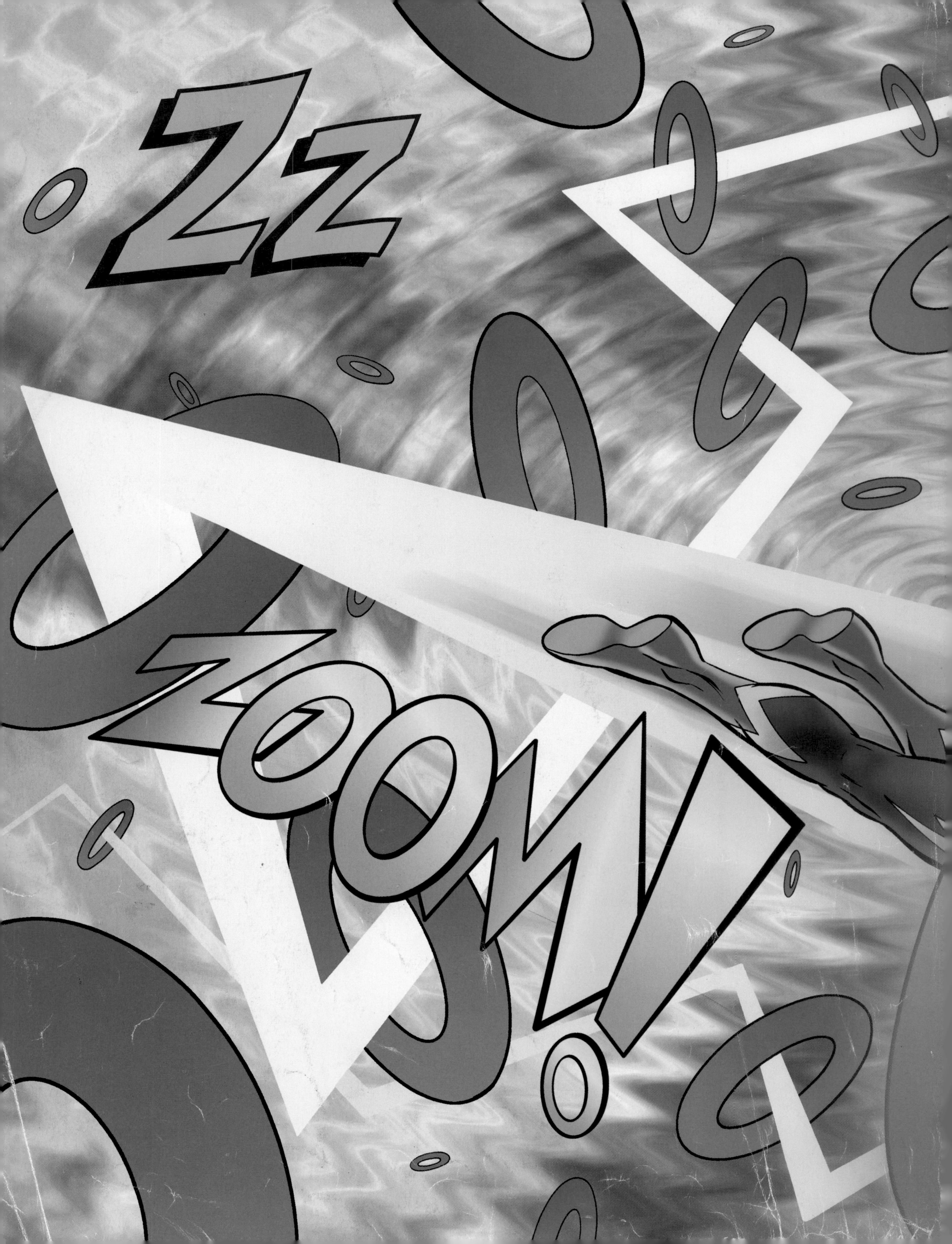
ZZ
ZOOM!

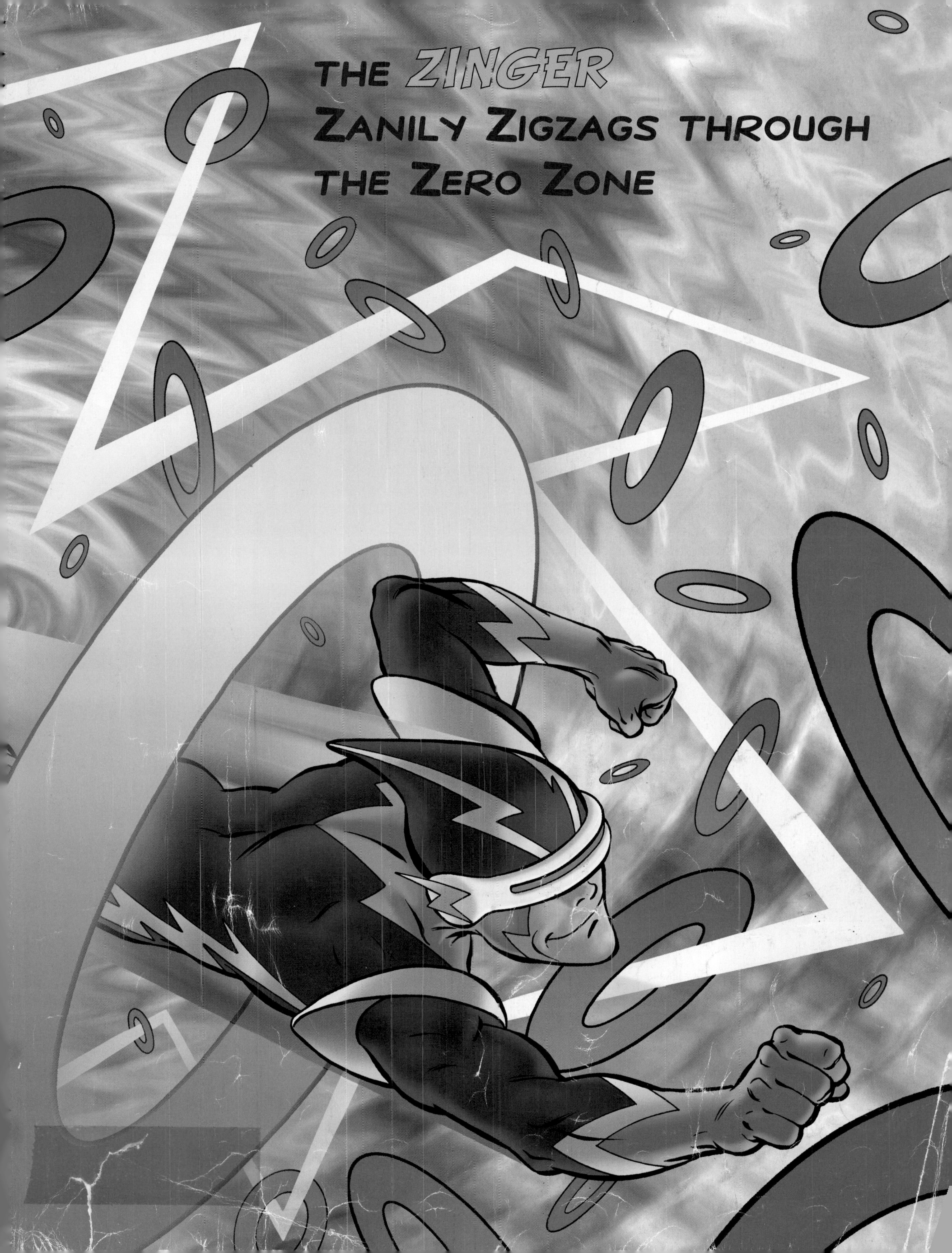
THE ZINGER
ZANILY ZIGZAGS THROUGH
THE ZERO ZONE

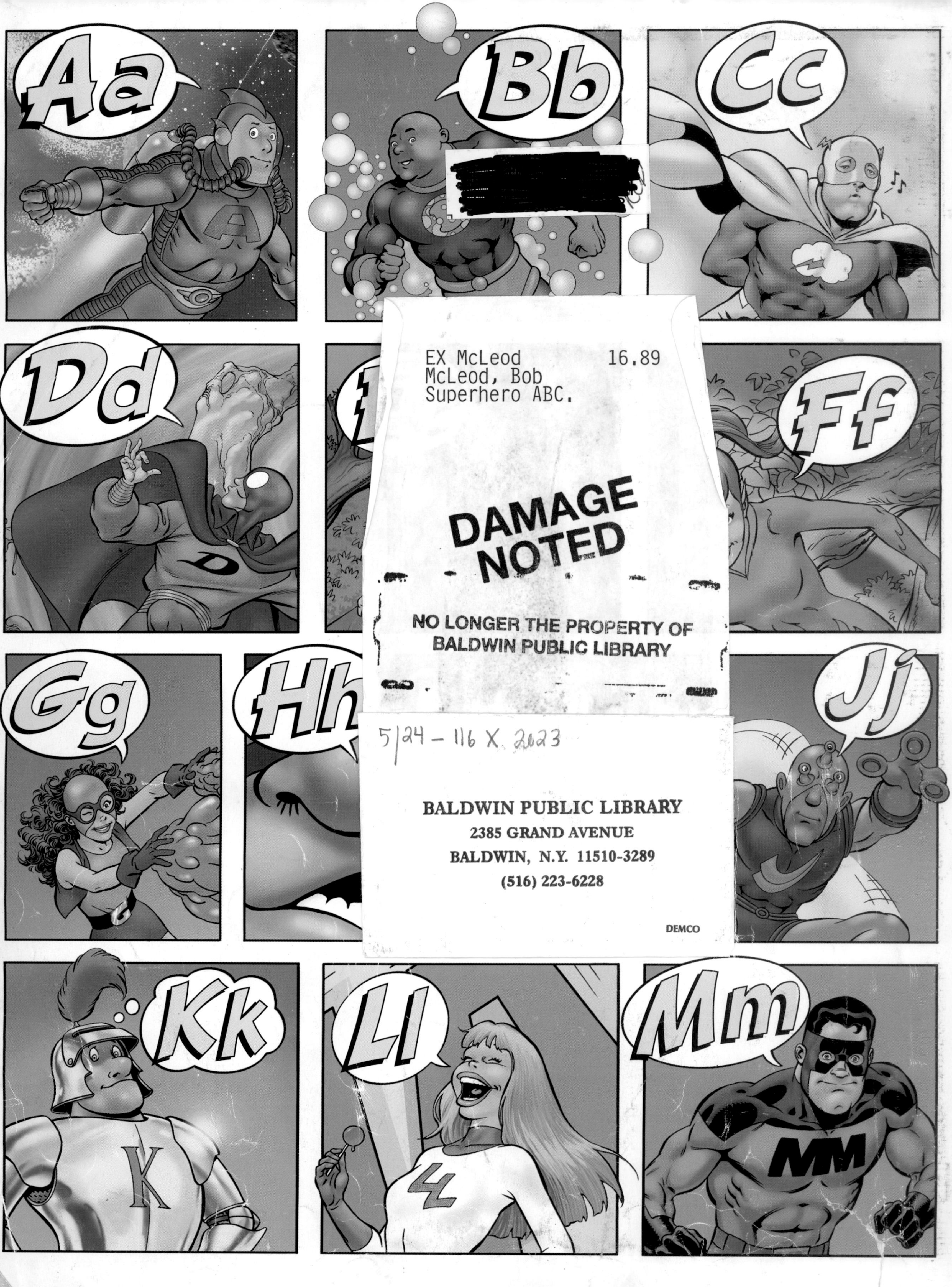
Aa
Bb
Cc
Dd
Ff
Gg
Jj
Kk
Ll
Mm